"Each of us, no ma... in life, can make a difference.

"Is that why you do what you do? To make a difference?"

"I like to think I am," Shelley said softly, at last. "Helping people who are in trouble. Sometimes I succeed. Sometimes I don't. But at least I know I've tried."

Caleb wasn't surprised at her answer. He was beginning to realize that Shelley Rabb was a special kind of woman. A warrior. A believer. She was all those things and more.

"For what it's worth, you're making a difference to me. To Tommy." He hesitated. "Why is that so important to you? Making a difference."

She didn't answer right away, and he wondered if he'd gone too far, asking something so personal. She stilled, as though searching her heart as to how much she should reveal, how much she wanted to reveal.

As a man who guarded his own privacy, he understood. Giving away too much of one's self left a person vulnerable. That was something Caleb had promised himself he'd never be.

Jane M. Choate dreamed of writing from the time she was a small child when she entertained friends with outlandish stories complete with happily-ever-after endings. Writing for Love Inspired Suspense is a dream come true. Jane is the proud mother of five children, grandmother to seven grandchildren and the staff to one cat who believes she is of royal descent.

Books by Jane M. Choate

Love Inspired Suspense

Keeping Watch
The Littlest Witness

THE LITTLEST WITNESS

JANE M. CHOATE

HARLEQUIN® LOVE INSPIRED® SUSPENSE

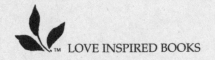

LOVE INSPIRED BOOKS

Recycling programs for this product may not exist in your area.

ISBN-13: 978-0-373-67729-0

The Littlest Witness

Copyright © 2016 by Jane M. Choate

www.Harlequin.com

Printed in U.S.A.

Be still, and know that I *am* God: I will be exalted
among the heathen, I will be exalted in the earth.
–Psalms 46:10

To all of America's servicemen and women,
past and present, especially those wounded warriors.
Thank you for your courage and service.
America owes you a debt that can never be repaid.

ONE

A muffled footstep awakened Caleb, setting him on high alert. There was no reason anyone should be here. No good reason, that is. Calmly, he slipped from the bed and stepped behind the draperies, just as an intruder entered the bedroom.

Another man might have panicked, but Caleb Judd was not just another man. Instinctively, he clicked into Delta mode, a heightened sense of awareness overtaking him, his vision sharpening, his hearing growing more acute. His breathing remained regular, his pulse steady, courtesy of training from the United States Army.

No one should have gotten in. Alfred Kruise had boasted about the state-of-the-art alarm system when he'd offered Caleb use of the guesthouse, insisting that both he and his nephew, Tommy, were safer here than they would have been anywhere else.

Kruise had been wrong.

The alarm system hadn't gone off. Probably disabled.

A pro.

The stranger's movements were nearly silent as he made his way toward the bed, his intentions clear. He wanted Caleb. But why? He had his share of enemies, but they weren't personal. Fighting his country's enemies was what he had been doing when he'd gotten the call about Michael and Grace's murders.

But now here he was in Atlanta, Georgia, eight thousand miles from Afghanistan, facing a gunman who clearly wanted to eliminate him. The only reason Caleb could think of was connected to his brother Michael, but that made no sense.

With his own weapon packed in his duffel bag, he had no chance of going for it. If he were going to take the man down, it would have to be with his hand.

Recognizing the disadvantages of his position, he relied on the faith that had sustained him through countless encounters with the enemy. It had never deserted him, even upon learning of the deaths of his brother and his wife.

Caleb registered the assailant's weapon held in a steady hand. A Walther. A good choice for an assassination. He'd probably appreciate it more if he weren't the intended target. He stepped out from behind the draperies and kicked out, knocking the weapon from the man's hand.

The would-be killer, who had to be several inches taller than Caleb's own six feet and weighed at least two hundred and twenty pounds, recovered quickly and grabbed for the weapon. Caleb spun, delivered a roundhouse to the man's chest, but fatigue and unrelenting grief had taken their toll upon him, making his effort lack its customary power.

The man gave a loud whuff. Caleb rammed a fist into the assailant's jaw. He must have had an iron jaw because he didn't buckle. The intruder pivoted on one foot and slammed the other against Caleb's chest.

Caleb dodged the worst of it but couldn't completely escape the punishing blow. He spun, presenting his profile, a smaller target for the next attack. The assailant had obviously had close-quarters combat training, since he didn't move away from Caleb's fists but, instead, closed in.

Just as the stranger raised his fist, a look of consternation passed over his face. And then Caleb noticed it. The man was wearing earbuds. Someone, a handler probably, must have been issuing orders.

After casting Caleb a look that promised retribution, the man took off. What had his boss said that had caused him to give up so easily?

He feared that the man realized he had the wrong target and Tommy was the intended one.

Caleb should have never left his nephew alone in the main house. Alfred and Irene Kruise had insisted it was best for Tommy, yet another instance where they had been wrong.

Whoever had sent a killer after Caleb might have also sent another after Tommy. But why? The boy didn't know anything. Fury built in his chest at the idea of anyone hurting Tommy. *Smother the rage*, Caleb told himself as he retrieved his weapon. He didn't have the luxury of giving in to it. Not now. Not when Tommy needed him.

Besides, there were bigger things he needed to concentrate on at the moment.

Three nights ago, Michael and Grace Judd had been gunned down in their own home while Tommy had watched. Caleb still shuddered at the thought of what his young nephew had endured. It was no wonder Tommy hadn't said a word since witnessing the shooting of his parents. Some grief was too deep for words.

The next few hours were a blur as Caleb had made arrangements to leave his unit in Afghanistan and fly to Atlanta.

He was beyond exhausted, at a time when he couldn't afford to make a mistake through a snap decision. One of the great ironies of life, though, was that in moments like these, snap decisions were all he had time for.

A different kind of fear settled in his heart. What was he to do with a seven-year-old boy? With no other family outside of a cousin, Michael and Grace had named Caleb Tommy's guardian in the event of the unthinkable. And now the unthinkable had happened.

Ideally, a child needed two parents, a mother and a father. Where was Caleb supposed to come up with a mother? With one bad experience under his belt, he had no desire to get on the romance merry-go-round again.

Impatiently, he shoved those worries aside. Right now he had enough on his plate, including staying alive and protecting Tommy.

With the weapon he had retrieved from his duffel held close to his chest, Caleb sprinted to the main house to check on the boy. The humidity of the Georgia night pressed against him, stealing the breath from his lungs, but he scarcely noticed. Nothing mattered other than keeping his nephew safe.

Silently, he admitted what he'd refused to acknowledge since he'd learned of the murder of his brother and sister-in-law: he needed backup.

Shelley Rabb lifted the heavy brass knocker and rapped it against the door to the guesthouse of the Kruise estate. Set in an exclusive neighborhood that shouted old money, the estate was a showplace, filled with dark, waxy magnolias, stone fountains and an air of gentility that had her wondering if she should genuflect before presenting herself.

Everyone in Atlanta knew of Alfred and Irene Kruise, who were featured on the society page of the paper at least once a week and were considered Atlanta royalty. Kruise was a federal prosecutor, and his wife sat on the committees of a half dozen or so charities. An invitation to the estate was a coveted ticket, although this wasn't exactly a social call. She was here as a favor to her brother, Jake.

"A buddy from Delta—Caleb Judd—called. He needs help," her brother had said in a phone call early that morning. "I wouldn't ask if it weren't important."

She knew that. Just as she also knew that she couldn't refuse. Jake was on his honeymoon with his bride, Dani. No way would she drag him from that, not after what he and Dani had gone through.

"I owe him, sis," Jake had said. For Shelley, that said it all.

If not for that, she wouldn't have taken the case. She had enough on her plate as it was, including handling the protection for a state senator who had received threatening emails from someone opposed to his stand on environmentalism.

But Jake had played the brother card, and the truth was, she'd do just about anything for him. She'd felt protective of Jake ever since he'd returned home from the Middle East, broken in body and in spirit. Love had made all the difference, and it had been Dani who had made him take those first steps toward trust and love. For that, Shelley would always be grateful to her new sister-in-law.

She straightened her blazer so that it hung smoothly over the SIG-Sauer 9mm she carried in a custom-fit shoulder holster, and prepared to lift the knocker again when the door was yanked open by a man who looked ready to do murder.

He matched the description her brother, Jake, had given her of Judd. "You're early."

"Is that a problem?"

"Yeah, it is," came the blunt answer. Annoyance had drawn lines in his forehead, but she sensed she wasn't the real target of his anger. "Come in." He pointed to a small room off the main hallway. "In there. I'll be with you in a minute."

Shelley narrowed her eyes. She didn't take orders. From anyone.

Setting aside her irritation, she opened a set of French doors leading to a small office and took a seat on a navy leather sofa.

The sound of raised voices caught her attention. Unashamedly, she listened. If there was one thing she'd learned in the security/protection business, it was that there were many ways to glean important facts, and eavesdropping was one of the best.

"You're making a mistake, taking Tommy away from here. This is the only place he's been safe since it happened." Frustration and worry sharpened a man's cultured voice. Alfred Kruise, she guessed.

"Last night proved that it's not safe." The words, though quietly spoken, held the unmistakable ring of authority, and she recognized the voice of the man who had answered the door.

"We'll tighten up security." The first voice grew more strident with each word.

"It's already settled. Tommy comes with me."

"You don't know what you're doing. Tommy is Irene's and my godson. We would do anything to protect him. *Anything*." A pause, followed by a tremulous sigh. "Michael and Grace were family."

"Maybe so, but I'm his guardian and I'm not leaving him here. I've already lost my brother and his wife. I'm not about to lose Tommy, too."

"Have it your way. I only pray you don't live to regret it." The slam of a door emphasized the other man's displeasure.

The man returned to Shelley. "I'm Caleb Judd." He gestured to the slightly built boy with dark hair and eyes at his side. "My nephew, Tommy." At Judd's nod, Tommy settled in a corner and pulled a couple of miniature cars from his pocket.

"Shelley Rabb."

Accustomed to sizing people up, Shelley studied S&J Security Protection's newest client. In a black T-shirt, dark jeans and Frye combat boots, he looked dangerous and deadly. In her job, she'd come across plenty of influential men, men who wielded the kind of power that came with money and connections and political clout. Caleb Judd carried a different kind of power, the kind that came from within. There was an underlying current of energy to him, and though banked now, that raw force was evident in how he moved and the clipped cadence of his speech.

His posture shouted his military background, as did his closely cropped hair. The tanned, weathered face had the hard lines of a man who did not spend his days in the office or the gym. And his battle-ready stance and sharp gaze were so like her brother, Jake's, that she almost did a double take.

Judd looked as out of place as she felt in the sumptuous surroundings. Score one for him.

"Thanks for coming." His words sounded as though he'd just gargled with cut glass, and Shelley winced at the pain underscoring them.

"Thank me when I've done something."

Shelley chose her clients carefully. S&J—her and Jake's initials—was her company. The clients didn't have to be wealthy, but they did have to be honest. At least with her. A recent client had been megarich, but he hadn't been trustworthy. She'd returned his retainer and suggested he find someone whose ethics were as challenged as his own.

The tightening of Judd's jaw and the impatient tapping of boots on the hardwood floor reminded her that he was Delta, a man who understood action. Still, she had a duty to him, as a client, and to herself, to make certain she could handle the job.

On a silent sigh, she acknowledged she was only postponing the inevitable. Of course she'd take the job. She didn't have a choice.

She looked into his blue eyes and resisted the urge to flinch when she saw nothing but ragged grief staring back at her. She supposed he might be considered attractive if his mouth were smiling. As it was, it was a hard line that compressed his lips together.

It looked as though he was holding himself together just as tightly. Tension radiated from him in palpable waves. From the harsh cast of his face and sleep-deprived features, he'd obviously gone through unspeakable pain since learning of the murders. But pain was not the only thing she read in his gaze. There was guilt, as well. She ought to know. She saw it every time she stared at herself in the mirror.

"I'm sorry," she said softly. "I can only imagine what you're feeling."

"Can you?" Judd retorted. "Do you know what it is to lose a brother?"

"I came close with Jake," she said, unoffended. "There were times when I didn't know if he would make it back."

Judd scrubbed a hand over his face, the rasping sound drawing her attention to the whiskers that darkened his jaw. She watched as he struggled to temper his voice. "Sorry. That was uncalled for."

"Don't apologize. We've got more important things to discuss."

"Like how I should have been there for him." Self-loathing coated his voice. "I told Michael he was in over his head. If he'd listened…if I had been there…"

She nodded to herself, confirming her earlier supposition that he was suffering from a crippling case of guilt. She didn't try to talk him out of it. Guilt exacted its own price in its own time.

Movements she suspected were normally smooth and economical were jerky, awkward, as though he didn't know what to do with the adrenaline instigated by fear and worry. "Jake told you why I need help?"

After making sure that the little boy wasn't within earshot, she turned back to Judd and answered in a low voice, "He said your brother and his wife had been killed and that you were attacked last night."

Other than the tightening of his mouth, Judd failed to react to the bald recitation of facts. He was probably in shock. The man had lost his brother and sister-in-law, had taken on the care of his nephew and had faced down a probable assassin, all within the space of a few days.

"You probably have the same questions I do," she said. "Was someone trying to kill you? Or just scare you off? What makes you a target?"

Judd didn't immediately answer. His gaze strayed to Tommy, who was still crouched on the floor, playing with his miniature cars. Of course his first concern was his nephew.

"I wish I knew."

Shelley paused. What was she doing, taking on a case that involved a child, a traumatized one at that? Every instinct in her told her that it was a mistake, but Caleb Judd had saved Jake's life. S&J owed him. *She* owed him.

And she always paid her debts.

Honor, plus an unwavering faith, was the cornerstone of how she conducted her life and ran her business.

She knew clients wanted promises that everything would be fine. She longed to give them just that. However, she couldn't give what she didn't have. If she'd learned anything in her years as a cop, then as an agent with the Secret Service, it was that life didn't come with guarantees.

Bad things happened to good people. She ought to know. The nightmare had resurfaced last night, and she'd beaten herself up over it, just as she always did. She'd awakened covered in sweat, guilt-laden and hurting.

She forced that aside and concentrated on Judd, who was rubbing two fingers above his nose as though to relieve a deepening headache.

A soldier's soldier was how Jake had described Caleb Judd. "The man doesn't have a single nerve in his body. He's totally cool no matter what's going on around him." Jake didn't hand out praise easily. If he vouched for Judd, that was good enough for her.

Judd wasn't looking totally cool now, though, she noted with a wave of compassion. He was beside himself with worry.

"I did some digging on the man your brother was prosecuting," she said. Upon promising Jake she'd provide security/protection to Caleb and his nephew until Michael and Grace's killers were caught, she'd crammed for this meeting, wanting to know everything she could find about the case. Caleb nodded impatiently, so Shelley took a deep breath and went on. "Jeremy Saba. He's never been convicted, never even been indicted. But he stands to go away for a long time if he's found guilty this time." Though Shelley had never worked on a RICO case before, she knew enough to understand the seriousness of the charges. "Is there anybody else I should know about?"

"One time Michael said something about a new player making a name for himself."

"Did he give you a name?"

"Ruis Melendez. My brother said he was a big shot in a Florida crime family."

Shelley digested that. "Anything else?"

Caleb shook his head.

She darted another concerned look in Tommy's direction, but he still appeared oblivious to what was going on around him. Nevertheless, she lowered her voice. "But even with your brother no longer on the case, nothing really changes. The charges still stand. So why target Michael?"

"Do you know how long it takes to build a case of this nature?" Judd demanded, his tone as sharp as barbed wire. "Michael got closer than anyone else to nailing this creep. Saba has to know that if he could get Michael off the case, everything slows down, maybe even comes to a complete standstill."

"I get that. I wondered if you did." Shelley nodded in satisfaction. "You're okay, Judd."

"So I passed?"

"Yeah. You passed." She gave a half smile. "Now you're wondering if I will. You don't know what I can do. I get that, too. I won't let you down."

His expression grew hard. "If you do, I'll cut you loose so fast your head will spin."

"Fair enough."

Still, she figured they'd better get the chain of command out on the table. "A couple of things up front. Nonnegotiable. When I give you an order, you do it. No questions asked. You do what I say. When I say. How I say."

If possible, Judd's mouth grew even tighter. "The other?"

"If things get rough, you don't go all macho on me and try to protect me just because I'm a woman. I'm the professional, and you're the client. I know you're Delta, but this is my op and I'm team leader."

He folded his arms over his chest but he nodded. "Agreed."

Shelley understood no man, especially a soldier, liked taking orders from a woman, but she had a job to do. She'd already made the mistake of allowing a man to tell her how to do her job. She wouldn't be doing that again. Not for anyone.

"Then we're good to go. Are you and Tommy ready to leave?"

"Yes."

She stood. "Let's do it."

"Where?"

She looked around the guesthouse, a haven,

she supposed, for some. It had not been a haven for Caleb Judd. "I'll let you know. Later."

A knock at the door had her tensing. Reason told her that an enemy wasn't likely to announce his presence that way. Still, she motioned Caleb to stay where he was. She withdrew her weapon, held it at her side as she answered the door.

A man in an austerely cut black suit, a starched white shirt, and a rigid bow tie stood on the front step and held an envelope. "Ma'am. This arrived for Mr. Judd. Mr. Alfred directed me to deliver it."

After slipping on latex gloves she'd pulled from her blazer pocket, she accepted the envelope. "Thank you."

Caleb joined her. "What is it?"

"It's addressed to you. Make sure Tommy stays in the other room." She started to open the envelope.

Judd stopped her. "My name. My responsibility."

The stern gaze he sent her convinced her to let him open it. Before she could hand him a pair of gloves, he'd torn open the envelope.

Inside lay a copy of a newspaper clipping with the headline Boy Dies in Pool and the crudely printed words *Back off or it could happen again*.

Shelley quickly scanned the clipping, inhaling sharply when she saw that it referred to Caleb's younger brother Ethan, who died before his second birthday. The accompanying note was a chilling warning.

She had taken this case because of Jake. But now that she'd met Caleb and Tommy, she was determined to protect them at all costs and go after the killers who had targeted them.

TWO

Caleb was grateful that Shelley hadn't interrogated him about the contents of the envelope, though he saw the questions in her eyes when she read about Ethan's drowning.

He wasn't up to explaining his role in the accident that had claimed his baby brother's life. Not now. Maybe Shelley would chalk up his silence to his concern for his nephew at the implied threat.

Caleb wasn't ready to relive the horror of that time in his life. He never talked about what had happened that day, the day that had changed his life forever. He shook away the memories and focused on the present.

Though her eyes had glittered with a take-no-prisoners ferocity, Shelley had remained calm and then called a friend at the Atlanta PD and explained the situation.

"One of my operatives will take the envelope to a friend in the Atlanta PD," she'd said. "He'll check for fingerprints, though I don't expect there to be any, especially after it's been handled by who knows how many people."

After the operative had shown up to retrieve the envelope, Shelley had hustled Caleb and Tommy out of the guesthouse and into her car.

Shelley Rabb's brown sedan was boring in the extreme.

Not so the woman, who couldn't be boring if she tried. Despite the black pantsuit she wore and her understated makeup, she was striking with her sleek dark hair and intuitive gray eyes that seemed to see right through him and strip away the protective layers he'd built around his heart. A smattering of freckles across her nose belied her otherwise professional appearance.

Shelley Rabb was a walking contradiction— understated, graceful, yet athletic, and, given her Secret Service background, lethal when and if the circumstances warranted it. She was no bigger than a minute, but she made up for it in the sheer determination that radiated from her. The severe pantsuit revealed a toned and disciplined body, despite her small size.

It was obvious that she downplayed her looks, another leftover from her years in the Service.

Caleb liked what he saw, but it was the energy she carried with her that caught and held his attention. Her no-nonsense manner coupled with a fresh vitality was like a brisk breeze that swept all other impressions aside.

Her background was evident in the way she moved, her arms swung slightly away from her body, a sign of someone who wore a gun for a living. If anyone looked closely, he'd see the outline of the weapon she carried beneath her jacket, but it wasn't bad camouflage. Caleb's own weapon, a Glock, was tucked in the waistband of his jeans with his shirt pulled over it. He missed the heft of his Colt M4A, a mainstay of the Special Forces, but the Glock made an acceptable substitute.

He hadn't missed her earlier study of him, the shrewd gaze which weighed words and expressions. Nor, he guessed, had his study of her gone unnoticed. It paid to know who you were working with, especially when lives were on the line.

Jake's recommendation not withstanding, Caleb had done his homework on Shelley. He hadn't realized that Jake was on his honeymoon until he'd called his buddy and Jake had suggested Caleb contact his sister. From all he'd learned, she was good at what she did. Great at it, if the glowing reports from clients posted on S&J's website were any indication.

"Rabb delivers the goods," one client, a CEO of an electronics company, had written.

Caleb returned his attention to the boring, nondescript car and wondered if she had chosen it precisely because it would attract little, if no, attention. A good choice for someone trying to become invisible.

Conversation was kept to a minimum. Caleb had a feeling that it had more to do with the lady's preference than it did with the SDR she conducted. He'd been on enough protective details to recognize the employment of a surveillance detour route. Though tedious, SDRs were necessary to make certain no one was following them.

They left the city, heading north, thick woods bordering the ribbon of highway. Shelley kept to the speed limit, another tactic, he guessed, to avoid attracting attention. Everything she did was low-key. The flashy moves one might expect from a Secret Service trained bodyguard were conspicuously absent.

His approval rating of the lady climbed steadily. Even so, he wasn't about to hand over the reins to a woman he'd just met. Shelley might call herself team leader, but when it came to Tommy's safety, Caleb was in charge.

He refused to compromise on that.

When mile after mile had flown by, Caleb roused himself enough to ask, "Where are we going?"

"A safe house Jake and I bought a year ago. We keep it for clients who need to keep a low profile."

"You mean clients with someone trying to kill them?" he asked dryly.

"Something like that."

The heat of the day had abated, if only slightly, and the evening slid into a purple-hued dusk. Caleb glanced at Tommy, saw that the boy's face was gray with fatigue. Caleb couldn't deny that he was exhausted, as well. After chasing off last night's midnight visitor, he'd spent the remainder of the night in Tommy's room, watching over his nephew while doing some research on the bodyguard.

As though Shelley had read his thoughts, she pulled off the road at a bland motel that would never earn a five-star listing. At the registration desk, she asked for adjoining rooms.

Inside, Caleb looked about the cheaply decorated room. A television was bolted to the fake paneling of the wall. Carpet that might once have been a light green was now faded to a sickly yellow. The puny efforts of the room's window air-conditioning unit scarcely made a dent in the late afternoon heat.

"Burgers and fries okay with you?" Shelley asked.

"Sure."

Shelley returned within ten minutes and placed a white paper bag, redolent with the smells of grease-laden food, on the room's one table.

"Thanks," Caleb said.

"No problem."

He opened the bag and pulled out a burger, then handed it to Tommy. "Seems I remember you could put away two of these," he teased, "and still have room left over for a chocolate shake."

Tommy made no comment but took the burger and began to eat automatically. Though Caleb tried to pull him into the conversation, the little boy only stared at him blankly.

Don't let him see your pain, Caleb told himself. *Keep it casual.* So he ate his burger and kept his worry to himself, praying Tommy's inability to speak was temporary.

Shelley, likewise, said little during the impromptu meal, leaving Caleb feeling as if he was talking to himself. Curiosity about his lovely bodyguard tugged at him. He knew the bare bones of her background. Ex–police officer and Secret Service agent. But he wanted to know who the lady was, why she did what she did. "What made you leave the Service?"

Her jaw slid to one side, as though she was considering her answer. "It was time to move on."

That told him nothing. From what Jake had relayed to him, she had been on the fast track to the presidential detail, the most coveted job in the Service. There had to be more to this story.

"Do you ever miss it?"

"Sometimes." She squared her shoulders and,

at the same time, lifted her chin, making it clear that she wasn't going to be expanding upon her answer. "I think we could all do with a rest. I'll be next door if you need me."

After her departure, Caleb put Tommy to bed. To combat the sweltering heat, he splashed water on his face. The unending grief was so heavy upon him that he scarcely recognized the features staring back at him in the bathroom mirror.

His eyes appeared sunken in a face churning with torment, scars grafted into the angles and planes. He fought against the desperation that soured his gut and the abject fatigue that threatened to draw him into a black pit.

Caleb pressed his fingers against his nose in an attempt to press back the pain, but some things could not be willed away. No matter how much he might want to. His knees nearly buckled.

Michael.

His brother's name echoed through Caleb's mind. "I'm sorry, little brother. I should have been there for you." His words came in ragged whispers, like worn-out remnants. "I should have been there for you," he repeated. "I should have been there for Ethan." He pushed memories of the little brother who had tragically drowned to the back of his mind where guilt couldn't flay his conscience raw. "I should have…"

Should-haves didn't count.

* * *

With a sigh of relief, Shelley withdrew to her own room. There was no sense in denying it: Tommy unnerved her. What was she supposed to say to a child who had lost both parents, who stared right through her as though she were invisible?

And what was it about the newspaper clipping that had caused Caleb to withdraw as he had? The death of a brother was horrible, especially when coupled with Michael's murder, but Ethan's drowning had been an accident.

Caleb's eyes had narrowed, his mouth assuming a tight-lipped expression that had warned her to keep her inquiries to herself.

There were too many questions and not enough answers. Later, she promised herself, she'd get the intel she wanted. For now, she, Caleb and Tommy needed rest.

Shelley stretched out on the thin mattress that managed to be both hard and soft at the same time and willed herself to sleep. In this business, you slept when you could because you never knew if it would be the last rest you'd get in who knew how many hours.

Two hours later, she heard it—a faint noise outside her door. The noise could be a stray cat or dog. She listened intently. There it was again. The snick of metal against metal, as though someone were trying to access the card-coded lock without the card.

Grateful she hadn't undressed, she slipped her shoulder harness back on and clicked the latch. Silently she made her way to the doorway connecting the two rooms, opened the door to Caleb and Tommy's room, and saw that Caleb was also dressed. He nodded, acknowledging that he'd heard the same noise.

She inched toward the window, did a turkey peek over the sill and saw two men with guns drawn. Crooking her finger, she gestured to Caleb to join her. The grim look in his eyes was confirmation that he understood they were under attack.

He was braced, his stance that of a warrior ready to defend what was his. The idea of running was foreign to him. At the same time, they couldn't afford a gun battle, not with Tommy in the room. Protecting an innocent child was what mattered now.

"We've got to get out of here." Her words sounded overly loud to her sensitized ears. "I'll go first." She pointed to the bathroom window above the toilet, indicated she would climb out, that Caleb should pass the sleeping Tommy to her. She wondered if Caleb's broad shoulders would fit through the narrow window, but there weren't a lot of options.

Another nod.

When she was on the ground, Caleb handed Tommy to her, then climbed out himself, angling his shoulders to make it through the opening. Once they'd made their escape, she pointed to the car, which she'd parked at the back of the motel.

Quietly, the threesome stole through the Georgia night. When they reached her car, Caleb started for the driver's seat.

She shook her head. "I'll drive. You see to Tommy."

A shout from the front of the motel alerted her that whoever had followed them had discovered they had escaped.

There was no more need for silence. Shelley yanked open the car door and slid behind the wheel. Caleb secured the seat belt around Tommy.

"You up for this?" she shouted as Caleb buckled himself in the passenger seat.

"Are you?"

"We'll see."

A black SUV with tinted windows, a cliché, Shelley thought contemptuously, rounded the corner. She punched the gas, took the driveway out of the parking lot and sped into the night. At the same time, she said a silent prayer, asking for the Lord's protection and help. She knew she couldn't do this on her own.

When she didn't immediately see the SUV

behind her, she allowed herself a small sigh of relief.

Then she saw it.

Another SUV, black like the first. She didn't bother hoping it was just a high school boy and his date out for a late night drive. No, this was the backup vehicle, and it was heading straight for them.

At that moment, the first SUV reappeared in her rearview mirror. A real-life car chase was nothing like what was portrayed on television. There was no dramatic music, just the relentless knowledge that the enemy was closing in. And unlike on television, there would be no hero riding to the rescue. If she were to get Caleb and Tommy out of this, she had to depend on herself. And the Lord.

"Make sure your seat belt is pulled tight. Then hold on." Breath hissed between her teeth even as cold sweat trickled down her back, signaling her body's response to stress. The reaction was physiological. Over the years, she'd learned to use it, releasing anxiety while allowing her to function at peak performance.

Shelley didn't bother making sure Caleb complied with her orders. She was up to her neck in crocodiles, or, in this case, SUVs, and needed all of her attention for the road.

The driver of the second SUV would expect her to slow down, perhaps to turn away. She did neither. Instead, she laid down some tread until the car was nearly adjacent to the SUV, the first in hot pursuit.

Tommy let out a startled cry.

It was a life-and-death game of chicken, one she was determined to win. Her smaller vehicle didn't have size or power on its side, but it had maneuverability, and, in this instance, that trumped size.

She didn't let up on the gas but punched it until she was mere inches from the second vehicle. She spared a glance in the rearview mirror and saw the first bearing down on her.

Good.

Close enough that she could see the startled expression on the driver's face, she nearly smiled. Would have, if the circumstances hadn't been so dire. At the last minute, she veered sharply, shooting the car around the SUV. Sweat, cold only moments ago, now burned through her shirt and blazer.

Shelley held her breath. Could she make it? She pushed that from her mind. She *had* to make it. Caleb and Tommy's lives, not to mention her own, depended upon her doing just that.

"Don't let up now," Caleb said. "Keep going."

Tires left pavement, bumping along the uneven ground, kicking up hunks of dirt and grass, until, with a twist of the wheel, she muscled her way back onto the road.

A screech of tires and the inevitable crash told her that her ploy had worked, the first vehicle ramming into the second with a satisfying crunch of metal and glass.

A grunt from Caleb and small sob from Tommy had her checking her rearview mirror once again. At Caleb's grim nod, she refocused on the road. They weren't out of the woods yet.

"Hold on," she shouted once more.

After she let up on the gas, she spun the wheel, then executed a perfect J-turn, one even her driving instructor at the Service would have given her full marks for.

While the occupants of the two SUVs scrambled out of their ruined vehicles and managed to get a couple of shots off, she came out of the one-eighty and had the car pointed in the direction she wanted to go.

She gunned it. With a squeal of tires and the spit of gravel, it shot forward.

"Jake was right," Caleb said. "You're the real deal."

Shelley didn't waste time responding. They'd managed to escape their attackers this time. But what about the next?

The fight wasn't over. It had just begun.

THREE

"That was some driving, lady." Caleb's voice cut through the night.

"Thanks. I think." Energy continued to pump through Shelley, even though the crisis was over, at least for the moment.

From habit, and need, she mentally repeated a scripture from Psalms: *Be still and know that I am God.* Calm flowed through her at the familiar words. Her breathing leveled, and her heart rate gradually returned to normal.

"Maybe we can go back another time and pick up my heart," Caleb added. "I think it popped out of my chest around the time you almost lost that game of chicken back there."

Shelley flicked a glance over her shoulder. "Liked that, did you?"

"I don't believe that's what I said," he corrected dryly.

The muted light of the dashboard revealed a hint of a smile in a jaw that was darkening with beard shadow. Once again she was struck by the masculine appeal of the man that managed to combine bold, rugged good looks with incredible blue eyes that could warm with tenderness when he gazed at his nephew or turn glacier cold when that same nephew was threatened.

She wondered what it would be like to meet him under normal circumstances. Nothing about the past twelve hours could be called normal.

While she appreciated his humor, Shelley was keenly aware of the chance she'd taken. Risking her own life was one thing; risking that of Caleb and Tommy was something else. But what choice had she had?

The protection/security business had only two rules. Rule number one: protect the client. Rule number two: refer to rule number one.

"I was praying the whole time," she admitted in a low voice.

"Me, too. A soldier quickly learns that prayer is the only real protection."

She stored that away, to be taken out and examined later. "How's Tommy?"

"He just keeps staring out the window," Caleb said.

She was no expert in child psychology, but she knew enough to recognize that Tommy was not responding in a normal manner.

"What's going to happen to him?" she asked

softly. "After this?" It was as if Tommy were in some kind of trance.

"I don't know," Caleb admitted.

"There're people who can help."

"I know. But first we have to protect him."

"And you," she added.

His nod was brusque. She knew his own safety mattered far less to him than that of his nephew. He glanced out the window at the passing scenery.

"How long until we reach this cabin of yours?"

"Another hour if we were going straight there. Which we're not."

"Care to enlighten me?"

"We're heading back to Atlanta to pick up another car. Those guys had to see what we're driving, maybe even the license number if they had infrared capabilities. Which I'm pretty sure they did. They've probably already reported back to whoever they're working for." She'd spent the past few minutes working things out in her head. Once it had stopped spinning, that is.

"How're we going to get another vehicle?" Caleb asked.

"I'm going to tag Sal, one of our operatives, to meet us with a car."

"Salvatore Santonni?"

"Yeah. He works with Jake and me. Did you two serve together?"

"I never had the honor, but I heard plenty. He's

got a rep for doing whatever it takes to get the job done."

Shelley allowed herself a small smile. "He's the best."

Caleb was silent for several long moments. "How did they find us?" he asked abruptly. "You're the only one who knew where we were heading." Was there a whiff of accusation in his voice?

When she didn't reply, Caleb had the decency to apologize. "Sorry. I know you didn't lead them to us. But how *did* they know where we were?"

"I don't know. But I intend to find out." Shelley prayed she could make good on that promise. The truth was, she had no idea how the men had found them at the motel.

She always checked her car for any tracking devices. Caleb had tossed his cell, and she had a burner, so there was no way anyone could ping their location from their phones.

Using her Bluetooth, she called Sal, explained the situation. "Thanks, Sal," she said when he agreed to meet her with a different car.

"We're set," she said to Caleb.

Twenty minutes later, she pulled into the parking lot of a convenience store where Sal was waiting with a blue minivan.

"Really?" she asked with a raised brow. "A minivan?"

Sal lifted a massive shoulder. "Who's going to look for you in a soccer-mom mobile?"

He had a point. She made the introductions and then watched as the two warriors acknowledged each other.

"It's a pleasure," Caleb said at last. "You're a legend."

Sal shook his head. "Nah. I'm just a good ol' boy. Jake tells me that you saved his bacon back in the day."

"Let's just say we took turns saving each other's bacon."

Sal slapped Caleb on the shoulder. "Don't I know it. Serving in the Sandbox, you learn who your friends are." His expression sobered. "I heard about your brother and his wife. I'm sorry, man. No one deserves that."

Grimacing, Caleb gestured to the backseat where Tommy slept. "Especially him."

Sal's mouth hardened. Shelley knew he had a soft spot for the innocents of the world. Jake had told her that his gentleness with children had earned him the nickname Gentle Giant.

"Yeah," he said thickly. "Especially him."

Caleb transferred Tommy from the car to the van. Tommy didn't stir but slept on, his soft snores adding an air of normality to the situation.

Shelley supposed they should be grateful that he didn't wake up, but she continued to worry about the boy's lack of response. An unwelcome childhood memory surfaced. When she'd turned ten, she'd finally accepted that her mother, who had abandoned Shelley and Jake years earlier, wasn't coming back.

For days, Shelley had shut down, going so deep inside herself that nothing had registered. The only thing that had pulled her out was Jake's tears. Seeing Jake, the big brother she adored, crying had shocked her to the core.

What would it take for Tommy to find his way out of the numbing pain that encased him?

Not her problem, she reminded herself. Her job was to protect Tommy and Caleb. Getting Tommy the help he so obviously needed was his uncle's responsibility.

"Thanks, Sal," she said. "Tonight you saved my bacon."

"All this talk of bacon saving is making me hungry. Be careful," he added with a tap to her cheek. "Good bosses are hard to find."

To Caleb's surprise, Shelley didn't immediately start the van after Sal drove off.

"We need to go through Tommy's things," she said.

"You think someone's put a tracker in his stuff?"

"It's one way of knowing where we're going practically before we do."

Together, Caleb and Shelley started going

through Tommy's belongings. Systematically, they searched his clothes and the few toys he'd brought with him.

"There's nothing," Caleb said in disgust thirty minutes later after they'd gone over each item twice. "Nilch. We're back to square one."

"You couldn't have told anyone," she mused aloud. "You didn't even know where we were going. I was the only one."

"Yeah." The suspicion was back. Shelley *was* the only one who knew where they were had been going. So how had the shooters found them?

His feelings must have shown on his face, for she said, "Hey, they were shooting at me, too. I'm not the target. *You* are." She paused. "That clipping was meant to scare you off."

"I'm sticking. I owe it to Michael and Grace."

How had anyone known about Ethan's accident? It had happened almost thirty years ago.

As she had on the first leg of the journey, Shelley performed multiple SDRs. It ate up valuable time, but Caleb understood the necessity. No one could have followed the convoluted backtracking and lane changes she employed without being spotted.

They reached the cabin three hours later. Fashioned of split logs and stone, the structure was a perfect complement to its rural mountain setting.

While Caleb carried Tommy inside, Shelley brought in their bags.

"There's a bedroom off that first door," she said, gesturing to a hallway. "You and Tommy can bunk in there."

"After what happened at the motel, I'd feel better if we all stayed together. In case…"

Shelley's nod was one of warm understanding. "Of course."

Caleb settled Tommy on a sofa, covered him with a throw he found on the back of a chair, then took the opportunity to check out the cabin. It wasn't spacious but looked comfortable and clean. The soldier in him approved of the compact size. Small was easier to defend and control than large.

After noting the location of windows and doors, he nodded to Shelley. "Looks good." He sat next to Tommy and then propped his feet on the stone coffee table.

"We're both exhausted," she said and sank onto a matching sofa. "Let's get some sleep. There're still a few hours before daylight."

But she didn't close her eyes. Neither did he. Adrenaline was still flowing through his bloodstream, making sleep impossible. He figured it was the same for Shelley. His thoughts were a quagmire of questions and self-recriminations. Like rowdy children, they refused to behave and leave him in peace.

Caleb didn't like wasting time, so he decided to use it to learn more about his savvy bodyguard. She'd been both cunning and bold in out-witting and outdriving the SUVs.

"Jake said you were a top scorer in shooting competitions in the Service," he said, recalling what Jake had told him about his sister. "Since the Service hires only the best of the best, that's pretty impressive."

Her elegant brow rose at his words, but she didn't confirm them, her lips folded so tightly together that there was no hint of softness there. At the same moment, something raw flashed through her gaze. The darkness behind her eyes hinted at something he hadn't expected. Sorrow. Regret. Guilt.

"You'd think so, wouldn't you?" she said at last. With those cryptic words, she turned away from him.

"Did I say something wrong?"

"No." But the word was muffled.

Caleb puzzled over her reaction. What had he said to make her stiffen up as she'd done?

Shelley came off as secure in who she was and what she did with her take-charge attitude and brash confidence. As much as he told himself he shouldn't be curious, he couldn't help wonder-ing why her eyes were so filled with shadows. Or had he imagined it because he was looking through his own veil of pain?

Not his business, he reminded himself. His

only business was in protecting Tommy and finding out who had killed Michael and Grace.

Caleb noticed his hands were fisted and forced himself to unclench his fingers.

Never had he felt so helpless, so powerless. That wasn't something a Delta soldier was comfortable with. Give him an enemy to defeat, a munitions dump to take out, a rescue mission to perform, and he was your man. He knew what he was doing in the field.

Time had given him regrets. It had also forced him to accept the truth about himself. He had deserted Michael when his brother needed him the most, not because he believed he could save the world—no soldier who had served believed that after the first day of combat—but because he was good at what he did. Because he relished the challenge. Because when he did the job right, he felt good about himself.

Was that so terrible to want to feel good about himself? His childhood had been spent knowing he hadn't measured up, would never be able to redeem himself after letting his baby brother die. Wasn't he entitled to have this one thing to feel good about?

He hadn't exactly deserted Michael, Caleb reminded himself. Michael had sent him away, the harsh words he'd uttered still echoing in Caleb's mind. It was scant comfort, though, when he struggled to accept that his brother was dead.

Forcibly, he pulled his thoughts from the mire of pain, and, without volition, returned them to the feisty bodyguard.

"You're staring," she said, and he realized she'd turned back to face him.

Her words jerked him back to the here and now, and he wondered if he'd imagined the roiling emotions he'd read in her gaze only moments ago. "Sorry. I was trying to get a handle on who you are."

"No problem." Shelley lifted a shoulder in a careless shrug, but the intensity in her lovely gray eyes belied the casual gesture. "What you see is what you get. Ex-cop, ex-Secret Service agent."

He had a feeling there was much more to Shelley Rabb than that. She thought fast on her feet, kept her cool under fire and didn't back down from a challenge. She said what she meant and meant what she said. The old saying described the woman perfectly. There was no pretense about her, but he sensed a well of pain beneath the no-nonsense exterior.

"What about you? You're Delta. What about the man under the soldier?"

Caleb had no answer to that, at least none that he was willing to share. He'd buried the part of him that wasn't a squared-away soldier long ago.

"Is there someone special?"

"Not anymore." The words were out before he could think better of them.

"What happened?"

"You ask a lot of questions, lady."

"Comes with the territory. If you don't want to tell me, say so. My feelings won't be hurt."

How did he explain what had gone wrong between him and Tricia to Shelley when he could scarcely explain it to himself? He'd met his former girlfriend on one of his rare leaves home. She was beautiful, intelligent, sophisticated. It was obvious that she was going places. And she wanted to take him with her.

Through an encounter with a buddy who worked in the private sector, Caleb had learned that Tricia had interviewed for a job with an oil company and that her getting the job was contingent upon his signing with the company, as well.

Not wanting to believe it, he'd confronted her.

"I'm sure your friend misunderstood," Tricia had said with the smile that had bewitched him into silencing the little voice that had so often told him she had been lying to him from the start.

"The only misunderstanding was in my believing that we had something real. I was just your ticket to a six-figure job."

"Darling, what difference does it make why they want you? We'll have such a great life," she said with forced gaiety. "You can name your own price. Security is a hot ticket in the business world.

"You did your time for your country. Now it's time to do something for yourself. You could go anywhere, do anything," she said with another winning smile. "Delta's holding you back. Together, we make an unbeatable team."

He'd shrugged off her hands and looked at her with something akin to revulsion. "That's where you're wrong. We're not a team. We never were."

Caleb had known it was over from the moment she'd lied to him. Without trust, there was nothing. He'd put his faith in the wrong woman. He wouldn't make that mistake again.

Shelley hadn't said anything while he took a stroll down memory lane, and Caleb resisted the urge to squirm under her unwavering gaze.

"It didn't work out, okay? I moved on." He shrugged, as if to say it hadn't mattered. But it had.

"You don't owe me any explanations."

"What about you?"

Her laugh was hollow, her smile congealed. "Let's just say it's complicated."

Complicated could mean a whole bunch of stuff, he reflected. But from her tone, it was clear she didn't want to share that whole bunch of stuff, so he swallowed his questions.

He figured Shelley would share when and if she was ready.

A chunk of silence slipped by as darkness enveloped him. Caleb didn't attempt to sleep during those quiet hours. Arms folded behind his head, he stared up at the ceiling. It didn't feel awkward to spend the time listening only to the soft sound of Tommy's breathing and to absorb Shelley's presence.

Despite her energy, she had a restful quality about her. He appreciated it, and it didn't take much figuring out to know why. His life was filled with noise and action, and though he had chosen that life, couldn't imagine another kind, he found solace in the quiet shared with this beautiful woman.

He wanted to reach out and stroke her cheek. The knowledge pulled him up short. He had no business thinking of Shelley in any role except that of bodyguard.

He shook off the uncharacteristic reflections and wondered at their next move. Shelley was a top-notch operative, but despite her prowess, the threat hadn't stopped.

His thoughts came to an abrupt halt. Why come after a seven-year-old boy? Because Tommy knew something? But he was certain Michael wouldn't have shared anything about his work with his son. So what made Tommy so valuable?

Caleb gave a snort of disgust. Speculating was worse than useless, especially when he lacked information. He was no closer to having any answers than he'd been a day ago.

His heart clutched. "Lord, what am I going to do?" he whispered hoarsely. His voice scratched against a throat raw from unshed tears, his words releasing more pain than he'd felt in a long time.

Not even in Afghanistan when his unit had taken fire from all directions and they'd lost three men had he felt so completely helpless. With incoming fire pouring from the surrounding mountains, he and his unit had sought refuge in the scant shelter of a rock overhang.

Slugs ricocheted off the rocks behind and to the left of him and his men, and Caleb felt bits of shrapnel striking all around him, deadly pellets that tore through and destroyed flesh. The machine guns had to be spitting out .50 caliber ordnance, each round the length of a man's finger and undoubtedly armor-piercing.

It wasn't hard to determine the weapons used against him and his unit, not with the supersonic sound made by the guns and the distinctive muzzle flash. And then there was the unmistakable vapor trail of a .50 caliber. Once you'd seen one, you didn't easily forget.

It was a slaughter. Only by the grace of God had he escaped with his life. Others hadn't been as fortunate.

Prayer had come instinctively from his lips then. As though in answer to that prayer, the reassuring sound of Browning machine guns opened up as American forces came to the unit's aid.

He'd made it through. Would he make it through his brother's death, as well? He honestly didn't know. The self-doubt was unaccustomed, but nothing he'd felt or done in the past few days was like him.

Michael had been everything that Caleb was not: quiet, patient, slow to anger. The qualities had served him well in his job as a federal prosecutor.

Caleb knew little about the case Michael had been trying, only enough to understand that it was a high-profile one. If anyone should have died, it should have been him, he thought bitterly. He was a soldier, one who put his life on the line every day. Not Michael, who had chosen the law as his way to fight for justice. The law was safe.

Or it should have been.

Despair moved within him, and, beneath it, like a toll of a church bell, came the pain. His grief was so dense that he felt as though he couldn't draw a breath, that his lungs had forgotten how to work. At last a wheezing gasp escaped his chest. He listened to the gurgling sound, an acknowledgment that he was still alive despite his doubts.

He looked up to find Shelley watching him.

Her softly spoken words surprised him. "Grief is a work that must be done."

Tension simmered in the homey room, skirted across the plaid rug and wrapped its way around Shelley. She couldn't move, pinned by the stark despair in Caleb's blue gaze. Her stare lasted a heartbeat too long before she looked away.

She realized how quiet she and Caleb had grown, how still they'd become. It was as if all the sound had been leached from the room.

A sob erupted from Tommy, breaking the silence. Compassion stirred within her, but she resisted the urge to go to him, though she longed to give him the comfort he needed.

Shelley understood grief. She understood loss and fear and heart-wrenching pain. She understood all of them and still didn't know how to offer comfort to the small boy.

"It's all right," Caleb murmured and managed to quiet Tommy, to soothe whatever nightmare had caused him to cry out, and soon the boy was asleep again.

This time it was Caleb who turned his back to her. Whether he was feigning sleep or not, she understood that there would be no more sharing now.

It was too dark, and she was too alone, even with Caleb and Tommy in the same room. Without warning, her mind filled with reel after reel of pain-filled pictures. Her mother looking at her with a contempt bordering on hatred. Her disastrous last assignment with the Service. Her inability to forgive herself coupled with her gut-wrenching despair.

The memories speared through her, opening up pockets of bewilderment, outrage and heartache.

She'd believed herself to be in love, only to find that the object of that blind devotion had deceived her in the worst way possible. Jeffrey's betrayal had cut to the core of her being. After that, how could she trust herself to know what was real and what wasn't?

Caleb hadn't confided the details of what had gone wrong in his relationship; then, neither had she. But she felt an affinity with him. Though it had remained unspoken, it was apparent that they both understood the importance of always moving forward, because if you remained in one place for too long, you risked being crushed by the weight of regret.

Her regrets came with two dead men, one she'd considered a friend, one she'd hoped to marry.

Still lost in thought, Shelley released a quavering breath. If they managed to find who had killed Caleb's brother and sister-in-law while keeping Tommy safe, would that allow him to forgive himself for not being there when his brother needed him? And if she helped him, would that make it easier for her to visit the graves of the two men who had died during the botched mission?

Or were they both chasing the impossible?

She shook off the questions that had no answers and closed her eyes. Thankfully, the nightmare didn't return.

The sun was barely making its ascent when she awoke with a start, Caleb's question drumming through her mind. How had the gunmen found them?

Caleb had stretched out on the floor, next to the sofa where Tommy slept. She swept her gaze over the big, ruggedly handsome soldier as he kept guard over his nephew, even in sleep.

She stood and padded to the table. Once more, she searched Tommy's belongings. She and Caleb had examined the contents of the backpack, but they hadn't looked at the backpack itself.

Now she did so.

Painstakingly, she went over every inch of it. It was then that she found it: a tracker, so small as to be nearly invisible, sewn into the lining.

The implications sank in immediately. Shelley thought fast. Were the men who were after Tommy and Caleb already on their way? She didn't want to wake the little boy and drag him from yet another safe house.

But could she afford not to?

An indistinct rustling from the outside caught her attention. A zing of apprehension jolted through her. It could be nothing, she told herself.

The woods where the cabin was nestled were alive with rabbits, opossums, raccoons and even a hungry bear or two. But every instinct was telling her to get Tommy and Caleb out of there. Those instincts had saved her life upon more than one occasion.

Hypervigilant, she listened closely and now heard the fall of footsteps. Careful to keep out of the line of sight, she crept toward the window. A man moved stealthily up the porch steps. A second followed.

"Caleb," she whispered as she shook him awake. "Get Tommy. We've got to get out of here."

He came to as she would. Calm. Alert. Ready to act. Or fight. "What's going on?"

"Two men...outside...found the tracker...there all the time."

To his credit, Caleb didn't waste time asking questions of her disjointed explanation.

"Take Tommy out the back door," she hissed.

"What about you?"

"I'm right behind you. Go!"

"Not without you."

"I'll catch up."

"We go together." His tone brooked no argument, and he carried his nephew into the bedroom, shutting the door behind him before rejoining her.

She didn't have time to argue with him. By now, the men were not trying for stealth.

The men burst through the front door. The fact that they didn't wear masks alarmed her more than did the military grade KA-BAR knives sheathed at their sides and the snub-nosed revolvers they wielded with casual expertise. They didn't expect anyone to survive.

"Remember…no one hurts the boy," one said.

Shelley revised her assessment. The men didn't expect her or Caleb to survive, but they had other plans for Tommy.

The first man advanced on her, the grim look on his face as foreboding as the weapons he carried.

Caleb faced off against the other opponent. He didn't wait for the assailant to make a move, instead snapping out his right arm in an arc and knocking the weapon from the man's hand. He followed up with a blow to the chest with the heel of his palm, knocking his opponent backward a couple of steps.

Before the intruder could regain his balance, Caleb threw a deadly combination of jabs and crosses to the face. So rapid were his punches that it was all the intruder could do to protect his head as Caleb rained down blows.

Another time, Shelley would have admired

Caleb's skill; now, she was too busy dealing with her own attacker.

The hard gleam in the would-be killer's eyes promised he wouldn't go down as easily as his teammate. "Let's see what you've got, little girl."

"Yeah." She let her teeth show. "Let's." Quick as a snake, she brought the edge of her hand down on the wrist of his gun hand, sending the gun flying. She moved in fast, hooked her right leg beneath his, toppling him to the floor. With scarcely a pause, he rolled backward and jumped to his feet.

He wasn't even breathing hard and looked as though he were enjoying himself. "That the best you got?" His mouth twisted in an ugly sneer.

She didn't bother with an answer.

He'd obviously had top-notch military training, and deflected her flying fists and feet with little effort. She feinted to the left, spun on one foot, then struck out with her right fist. It connected with a bone-jarring crunch to his jaw. Pain sang up her arm.

She spun, hitting his throat with the toe of her boot.

He groaned but didn't go down and withdrew his knife from its scabbard, the honed edge gleaming menacingly. She had to stay out of its reach, and, at the same time, take him down.

Knives were a man's weapon, requiring skill, strength and, above all, reach. Though she was skilled enough with a blade, she lacked the necessary power to be really effective. Instead, she relied on moves that Jake had taught her.

When the man reached for her throat, she drove the ball of her hand upward under his nose. His agonized cry told her she'd broken it.

Good.

But self-congratulations were premature. He was still standing, still a threat. He swiped his hand across his nose, scowling when it came away bloody.

"You'll pay for that."

He shifted position, and she saw her opening.

"No. But you will."

She kicked out with her leg, striking his knee, causing it to bend in a way nature never intended. The knee, a particularly sensitive spot in the body, was crucial to standing, to movement, to balance.

Injuries to the knee could reduce the toughest of men to howling babies. Her assailant was no different. He screamed in rage and pain as he crumpled to the floor, clutching his injured leg.

"This ain't worth it," he muttered, spittle flecking his face. "Nobody said she was some kind of ninja."

"Better than ninja," she said and delivered the final blow to the back of his neck.

Shelley and Caleb made short work of tying up the assailants with zip ties she carried in her backpack. But she didn't delude herself into believing that this would put an end to the threat to Caleb and Tommy, if anything, she was more worried than ever. The enemy had upped the stakes, making it clear that Caleb was expendable. Even more chilling, what did they have in store for Tommy?

FOUR

"When do you leap over tall buildings in a single bound?" Caleb drawled as they sped down the highway after Shelley had hustled them out of the cabin.

The Georgia countryside was a blur as Shelley coaxed the minivan to maximum speed. If he weren't mistaken, they were heading back to Atlanta. After settling Tommy in the backseat, asleep with his stuffed bear in his arms, Caleb had climbed in the passenger side. He didn't like not driving, didn't like turning over that control. But clearly Shelley believed she should drive, so he held his tongue. Barely.

A dark cloud smeared the sky gray. The humidity was thick enough to slice and serve up on a platter. Much as Caleb had detested the sand that blew with unrelenting persistence in Afghanistan day and night, he preferred that to the clamminess that crawled over his skin now like a million wet ants.

She flashed a grin his way. "Haven't perfected that skill yet. I'll let you know when I do."

"Seriously, is there anything you *can't* do?" He ticked items off his fingers. "You drive like a NASCAR champ. You take down a man who's twice your size. I was beginning to feel as useless as a snowball in Alaska."

Her smile died. "I told you to grab Tommy and get out."

"You really think I'd leave you to take out two armed men by yourself?"

"Your first responsibility is to your nephew."

"Don't preach to me about my responsibilities," he said, voice cold as the desert night in Afghanistan he had only moments ago been feeling nostalgia for. "I'm well aware of my duties." Duty had defined him for as long as he could remember. Now it lay with Tommy. And it terrified him.

"Then why didn't you go? I can handle myself."

"So I saw. But Deltas don't leave anyone behind. Ever." The lash in his voice was unlike him. He chalked it up to a combination of fear, exhaustion and worry, but it was guilt that nagged at him unmercifully.

Ignoring his tone, Shelley retorted, "I'm not just *anyone*."

"Duly noted." He turned slightly so that he could see her profile. The softness of her features was belied by the firmness of her jaw. "You handled yourself like a pro back there."

"I *am* a pro, Judd. Get used to it."

Caleb didn't argue. He had met Shelley less than twenty-four hours ago, and in that space of time, she'd spirited him and Tommy out of a motel, engaged two SUVs in a deadly game of chicken, then taken down an armed assailant who was bent on killing her and Caleb.

She had done all this with such dispatch that he could only marvel at the woman's skill and courage. She was the real deal.

She hadn't drawn her weapon. He had a pretty good idea why, but he asked anyway. "Why didn't you use your gun? You had an opening."

"I would have if I'd needed to, but I figured the police will have plenty of questions for those yahoos. There's a chance they may even answer," she said, confirming his guess. "Plus, taking a life, even when it's justified, changes you. I didn't need that. Not again."

Caleb didn't mind using his gun. But, like any soldier who understood what that meant, he liked *not* using his weapon better. Then the last part of her comment registered. He shot her a questioning look, but she only shook her head.

After securing the gunmen with plastic flex-cuffs she'd pulled from her backpack, she'd called Sal and directed him to call the local police and have the men picked up. She'd fished in the men's pockets and had come away with nothing. "It figures."

"What?"

"No ID. Not even a burner phone to tell who they called last."

Caleb understood what she meant. There was no way to know who was giving the orders.

At that moment, a deer leaped from the woods, bounded over the guard rail and onto the road. Shelley braked sharply, avoiding the animal by mere inches. "Do you know that Bambi kills more people every year than Smokey the Bear?"

"I've heard stories."

The clouds of earlier spilled forth in a drizzle, which quickly turned into a heavy rain. With the beat of the rain a counterpoint to his thoughts, Caleb tried to digest the events of the past day and a half. Questions swirled in his mind, questions that led only to a quagmire of more questions. Nothing about this made sense. If the killers thought Tommy could identify his parents' murderers, why hadn't they disposed of him when they'd killed Michael and Grace? Why try to kidnap him now?

They rode in silence for thirty minutes until Shelley broke it. "I was afraid of this," she said, gesturing to what appeared to be an accident scene just ahead.

He got it immediately. An accident on this isolated stretch of road was too much of a coincidence to ignore. The punch of fear was not for himself, but for Tommy. "We're not stopping." He made a statement of the words.

"You got that right." Her smile was hard and tight. "You boys better say a prayer."

Shelley gunned the engine and maneuvered around the so-called accident. Angry shouts ensued, followed by the sound of car doors slamming and the roar of an engine.

"They're on our tail," Caleb said.

She didn't bother answering.

The road narrowed just ahead in a series of sharp curves. The rain had worsened, sheeting down the windshield and making visibility a wishful thought.

Gunshots rang out, peppering the rear of the van like a swarm of angry bees.

Caleb twisted in his seat, stuck his head out the window and fired off two shots. The shatter of metal hitting glass told her that he'd hit the windshield. She'd expected no less.

He was Delta, after all.

In a Hollywood thriller, he would have shot out the tires, but this wasn't Hollywood, and shooting out a tire from a speeding vehicle wasn't as easy as the movies made it look. In fact, it was nearly impossible.

Caleb looked over his shoulder. "That slowed

them down, but they're still coming." His grim tone echoed her own apprehension.

"I know." They approached a sharp curve. She made the turn too swiftly, cut the wheel in the opposite direction, and realized she'd overcorrected. A rookie mistake. For a few breath-stealing moments, the van spun out of control.

At any other time, she'd have wrestled the vehicle back on the road, but the tires failed to gain purchase on the rain-slick asphalt, sending them skidding to a hard stop against the safety railing.

The impact sent Shelley hurling forward, but the air bags cushioned the blow for Caleb and herself. That was both good and bad news, as the deployment of the airbags meant that the vehicle was now disabled. She glanced in the rearview mirror at Tommy, noted with relief that he appeared okay.

"Get Tommy," she yelled to Caleb and jumped out. "We've got maybe ten seconds before they're on us."

With Caleb carrying Tommy tucked under his arm, they ran for the trees as the pickup bore down on them and plunged into the dark greenness. The woods could be an unfriendly place, but they were a refuge now. The heavy smell of moss, wet leaves and soaked clothing swam through her senses.

The second the three of them hit the trees, bursts of gunfire sounded. With his free hand,

Caleb grabbed Shelley's arm. He dove and rolled, somehow managing to take both Tommy and Shelley with him until they were hidden beneath the dense underbrush of kudzu and ivy.

In the scramble of arms and legs, her ankle twisted beneath her. She didn't have time to worry about it as she worked to make herself as small as possible.

The darkness was their friend, as was the storm, no matter how wretched the cold and wetness were. No light found its way through the forest where each tree struggled to find a wedge of sunlight at the expense of its neighbor.

With a finger to his lips, Caleb motioned Shelley to keep quiet, though the reminder was hardly necessary.

The gunmen trampled through the thickly wooded area, their voices loud in the otherwise still air.

"We ain't gonna catch them now," one of them said, disgust ripe in his voice.

"The boss isn't going to be happy." The second man swung his arm through the bush, coming within inches of where Shelley lay hidden. He was so close that she could see the brand of sneakers he wore.

"I'd like to see him do any better," came the heated reply. "Are there snakes in these woods? I can't stand snakes."

"Suck it up. The boss wants the kid real bad."

"Well, he ain't gonna get him today."

The two men argued back and forth for another few minutes. They made another halfhearted attempt at beating the bushes but eventually gave up.

Shelley didn't let out her breath until the men had passed by where she, Caleb and Tommy were hiding.

Caleb motioned to Shelley and Tommy to remain where they were. "I'm going to follow them," he whispered in her ear. "I wouldn't put it past them to pretend to leave, then circle back."

She'd had the same thought, but it was her job to protect Caleb and Tommy. "I'll do it." She couldn't keep the stiffness from her voice.

With his face only inches from her own, Shelley made out the cold composure and resolution in his features, the anticipation of the hunter barely concealed beneath the surface.

"You know E and E?" he asked.

Shelley recognized the shorthand for the evasion and escape part of SERE's training. Though she hadn't had the same training in survival/evasion/resistance/escape that Deltas underwent, Jake had taught her enough that she wasn't a total novice.

Not waiting for her answer, Caleb melted into the deepening shadows of the woods. He moved so quietly that she didn't hear even the crack of a twig or brush of a branch. He was in warrior mode, she recognized, his instinct to defend, to protect, on full alert.

Alone with Tommy, Shelley took a moment to assess her condition. Her hands and arms were scraped and bloody, but nothing serious. More troubling was her ankle, which was beginning to throb.

Shake it off, she told herself. Except that she couldn't very well shake off anything when she was supposed to stay as still as possible.

Though it caused her stomach to do a jittery dance, she drew Tommy close. He neither resisted nor welcomed her embrace. It unnerved her that he remained so unresponsive. Anger welled inside her at the men who had traumatized an innocent child to the point that he couldn't even cry out in fear.

How were they supposed to fight an enemy with seemingly unlimited resources? A foe vicious enough to gun down a father and a mother in front of their son. How could such an enemy be defeated?

Shelley had seen her share of death, had witnessed the violence gang members visited upon each other with careless cruelty, but never had she encountered the scope of organization and communications network these killers possessed.

Every time she, Caleb and Tommy escaped one set of killers, another set popped up. It was time to try a different tack. She had an idea about that, if only they could get out of these woods alive.

All of this went through her mind as she huddled in the brush, praying that their pursuers had given up and that Caleb returned shortly. Much as she hated to admit it, she liked knowing he was close by.

Minutes ticked by.

Caleb returned, as silently as he'd vanished. "All clear."

Shelley drew a silent breath of relief, not recognizing until that moment how anxious she'd been while waiting for him. That annoyed her more than she wanted to admit. She wasn't some helpless damsel who needed a man to rescue her.

"It took you long enough." The snap in her voice annoyed her further.

He slanted a curious glance her way but didn't respond to her jibe.

"That was close," she said at last.

"Too close," he agreed.

His face was a scant inch from hers as he knelt to help Tommy and her from their crouched positions. Time hung for what seemed an eternity as Caleb held her gaze.

A shiver coursed through her.

"The van's toast, even if we dared return to it," she croaked, wanting, needing, to break the spell and bring some semblance of order to her scattered thoughts. "Which we don't." She squared her shoulders and resolved not to think about her injured ankle. Or the *thing*, she didn't know what else to call it, that had just passed between her and Caleb.

She climbed out from the bushes, winced as her ankle gave way. It was most likely twisted, maybe sprained.

Fortunately, Caleb had turned away. The last thing she wanted was for him to know she was injured.

FIVE

If it had been only himself to consider, Caleb would have gone on the offensive, taking on the assailants, but he had Tommy to consider. His nephew had to come first. Evasion was the order of the day.

His mind sifted through details about the men who had run them off the road. They were clearly the second string brought in only because the first had failed to complete the mission. Everything about them, from their heavy aftershave to their constant bickering while searching, marked them as amateurs.

Pros would have left off the aftershave and maintained strict silence while conducting a grid search.

Caleb chafed at the knowledge that he couldn't take them out, every fiber in him protesting the decision he'd been forced to make. He liked to hunt. He didn't like to be the one who was hunted.

No Delta did.

He picked his way over fallen trees and vines that snaked over the forest floor, ready to trip the unwary. Out of habit, he walked on the balls of his feet, the spongy ground absorbing any sound. The pungent odor of rotting vegetation was ripe in the air. Birds cawed and chirped, sending out warnings of an intruder's presence.

The smells and sounds took him back to conducting an op in Central America. Though the terrain was jungle rather than forest, the atmosphere was much the same: thick and damp and dark.

Caleb had worn a Ghillie then, a camouflage suit of burlap and Cordura. Each man in the unit had personalized his Ghillie, covering it with mud, dirt and whatever else he could find to mask not only his appearance but also his scent.

Nothing gave away a man's presence more than the smell of deodorant or soap or aftershave. Once, Caleb had lain in the midst of a group of guerilla rebels, and not a one of them had seen him until he'd risen from the jungle floor, a green-and-brown figure ordering them to drop their weapons and raise their hands.

Tommy had given out after the first mile, and Caleb was now carrying him. He turned back to where Shelley was trailing farther and farther behind.

He frowned. "You're limping." It came out as an accusation. Why hadn't she said anything?

"Yeah. So what?" With a few more steps, she caught up to him and Tommy and leaned heavily against the trunk of a tree.

He dipped his head toward her foot. "What happened?"

"I twisted my ankle."

"When I threw you into the woods?" Why hadn't he realized she'd been hurt?

She took a breath, tiny lines of pain bracketing her mouth. "Maybe."

"Why didn't you say something?"

"And accomplish what? We can't stop. You can't carry me. So we keep going." She made a face. "Besides, complaining is for wimps."

"You're no wimp." Why did everything he said sound like an accusation? "You're going to fall on your face in another minute."

"Give me some credit, Judd," she snapped. "I'm not some Southern miss who's going to swoon in your arms because I have an owie."

He let out a hiss of exasperation. "I never said you were."

"Don't worry. I'll keep up."

"That's not what I said."

"Did you stop whatever you were doing in Delta because one of your team had a boo-boo?"

"Of course not, but—"

"Then give me the same respect and let me take care of myself."

"Have it your way."

Caleb turned his back to her and resumed walking. If he slowed the pace a bit, well, he was carrying an extra sixty-five pounds, wasn't he, conveniently ignoring the fact that he'd carried much heavier weights for much longer times. It had nothing to do with Shelley's injury. Nothing at all.

Within another hour, it became obvious that they weren't going to make it out of the woods anytime soon.

Shelley's pace had slowed to a near crawl. Though she hadn't said anything, and he figured she'd die before she'd complain, the labored breaths she took told their own story.

He assessed the circumstances as he would any op, his brain already starting to break down the situation. Consider the options. Weigh the pros and cons. All in under thirty seconds. Deltas were trained to act quickly and decisively. A delay of even a minute could cost lives.

He scoured the area for snakes. A couple of his fellow Deltas had been afraid of snakes, though they'd never admitted to it. One had almost died from the bite of the deadly coral snake. He'd survived, only to die when an IED had exploded beneath his feet three months later.

A buddy had died, and Caleb had walked away

without a scratch. There was no good reason for it. His friend had done nothing wrong, and Caleb had done nothing particularly right.

It was the capricious nature of war that was often the hardest to accept. Why did one man die and another live? *Why him and not me?* Caleb had given up asking the questions because he had no answers, just as he had no answer as to why Michael and Grace had been murdered.

Impatient with the rambling thoughts, he concentrated on the current problem, namely getting Tommy, Shelley and himself out of these woods in one piece.

Satisfied that there were no snakes about, at least in the immediate area, Caleb set Tommy down and began gathering branches.

"Aren't you a little old to be working on your Eagle Scout?" Shelley asked as she eased down by Tommy, though not too close. Her voice was pitched at a normal level, but he heard the underlying strain. He didn't glance up from where he was weaving branches together.

"It may be summer in Georgia, but you and Tommy are both shivering."

She looked as if she wanted to object but then thought better of it.

"We can't go any farther." Using several sturdy vines, he lashed the lattice covering to some tree trunks, fashioning a poor man's shelter. "It's not much, but it'll keep out the worst of the rain."

He picked Tommy up and placed him inside the shelter, then did the same for Shelley before she could guess his intentions. Now for the hard part. "I have to leave you and Tommy. I need to find us a ride."

Her sharp intake of breath told him how she felt about that. "Yeah? How you gonna do that?"

Her flippant tone didn't fool him.

"I'll get to the road, hitch a ride, then find us something."

"I can make it." The tilt of her chin nearly made him smile.

"Prove it."

She scooted out of the shelter, stood and would have fallen if he hadn't caught her. Their eyes locked as a look of awareness passed between them.

He eased her back down, brushed his knuckles over her cheek. "I'll be back. Count on it."

What did it say about her, Shelley wondered, that facing down two armed men terrified her less than tending one small boy? Well, she'd tackle this mission as she would any other. With equal parts prayer and determination.

Except this wasn't any other mission. This was a seven-year-old child who was already so damaged he couldn't speak.

This mattered. A lot.

"I guess it's just you and me." Did that thin, squeaky voice belong to her?

Though she couldn't see Tommy's expression, she felt his curiously flat gaze upon her. What little light there was had been effectively doused by the woven roof over their heads.

"We'll be okay," she said, more for her benefit than for his. "Your uncle will be back soon."

Still no response.

Okay. She could do this. So why was her stomach tied into knots that even a Boy Scout couldn't unravel? She swallowed back her fear and set her jaw.

Caleb Judd may have been Delta, but he'd find that she could hold her own.

Hoo-yah.

Shelley kept her weapon close, its presence comforting. It wasn't unheard of for bobcats or even the occasional bear to roam these woods, and even though bears didn't usually attack people, she wasn't about to take any chances.

In his sleep, Tommy had snuggled closer to her, his head lolling on her shoulder, his arm slung over her. The sensation was not unpleasant.

She shifted slightly, the better to hold him close. They were wet and chilled. The canopy of trees prevented any sunlight from reaching them. In addition, there was the problem of their soaked clothing, which trapped the cold in.

Although it sounded ridiculous, they were in

danger of hypothermia. All she could do was to wrap her arms around the little boy more tightly and pray that Caleb returned quickly.

Though how he was going to get a car, she didn't know. And he still had to traipse back through the woods for her and Tommy. If he didn't return… She wouldn't go there.

Dear Lord, she prayed, *we could really use Your help. I know Your love is infinite, especially for children. Please protect this child.*

Prayer said, she assessed the situation. She was injured but far from helpless. She pulled her bag to her, rummaged through the wet clothing for anything remotely dry.

There. A jacket stuffed at the bottom of the bag had escaped the worst of the rain. The fabric was lightweight, but it would provide an extra layer of warmth. She drew it over Tommy, tucking it around him. With a smaller body mass, a child lost heat more quickly than an adult.

As for herself, well, she figured a little shivering would do her good. It might shake off the extra five pounds she wanted to lose. Her eyes closed. The activity of the past day and a half was catching up with her. It wouldn't hurt to rest for a few minutes.

As soon as the thought formed, she rejected it. She needed to remain alert. Tommy was in her charge. Falling asleep on the job wasn't an option. Ever.

It wasn't lost on her that Caleb had taken over. Her ego wasn't so fragile that she was threatened by that. Of course, she wasn't. He was a natural born leader, but when he returned, she would have to remind him that this was her op and that she was team leader.

As before, Caleb made no sound as he returned.

"Good. You're here." Was there a whiff of humor in his voice?

"You expected me to go somewhere?" The tartness was as much for her as for him. She needed to remind herself that he was a client. Nothing more.

"I come bearing gifts."

He held out a plastic bag. In it, she found bottles of water and a package of pain relievers. Gratefully, she popped out two pills and swallowed them down with a long swig of water.

His smile came and went. "Thank you. For taking care of Tommy."

"All I did was put a jacket over him. No big deal."

"Yeah." But the look he gave her was warm with appreciation.

She ignored it. Or tried to.

The problem of her ankle still remained, and she gritted her teeth as she thought of the trek out of the woods.

She scooted back beneath the canopy of leaves.

"One more thing." From the bag of supplies, Caleb removed an elastic bandage.

"You thought of everything," she said wryly.

His hands were gentle as he probed her ankle, then wrapped it. "I don't think anything's broken. Probably sprained."

"Yeah." She pulled on her sock and shoe. The ankle still hurt, but she could tell a difference already. "Seriously. Thank you."

"You're welcome."

Normally, Caleb was good at compartmentalizing his feelings, but, at the moment, the skill eluded him.

He yanked his thoughts away from the picture Shelley and Tommy had made huddled together and turned to a conversational cliché: the weather. "The clouds are moving out, but in the meantime, we're probably better off where we are. At least we won't get drenched."

She nodded.

He helped her hobble back to the makeshift shelter and climb inside. He squeezed his large frame inside as well and drew Tommy to him.

"You got more than you signed on for with this job. Why'd you take it?" He'd been wondering about that from the beginning.

"I owed Jake, and he owed you."

"That's it?"

"I always pay my debts." She angled her chin.

"Jake told me that you were one of the good guys. He doesn't hand out praise easy."

The words warmed Caleb's heart. "I wouldn't have made it without him."

"He says the same."

Caleb didn't know what Jake had shared with his sister about their time in the Sandbox, but he suspected his friend had told her enough that she knew something of what they'd endured.

It wasn't the memory of the heat or the sand or even the sound of enemy fire that crawled up a man's spine in the middle of the night and strangled his dreams. It was the faces of fallen comrades that haunted him.

He suspected it always would.

Guilt that he had survived and others hadn't ate at him even now. Nightmares caught him unaware, and he'd awake in a cold sweat.

The army shrink had told him to forget it and move on. Caleb didn't blame the man, who was both overworked and overwhelmed with the number of soldiers returning home wounded in body and spirit.

The irony was that Caleb didn't want to forget. He only wanted to learn to live with the memories, both good and bad. He figured that was what Jake was struggling with as well, accepting what had happened and learning to deal with it the best he could.

Sometimes, Caleb reflected, his best wasn't nearly good enough. Not good enough at all.

Shelley's voice yanked him back to the present. "Taking a trip down memory lane?"

"Something like that."

"Some things are better forgotten."

"And some things can never be."

The understanding in her eyes invited him to share, but he wasn't in a sharing mood.

She peered out from beneath the canopy. "Looks like it's clearing up."

Caleb crawled out, stood, stretched. They had some distance to go before they reached the truck he'd parked at the side of the road.

Shelley and Tommy followed behind him. "The sooner we get out of these woods, the better. There's no way of telling if those creeps who ran us off the road are coming back once the rain's stopped."

He nodded. The same thought had occurred to him.

With Caleb carrying Tommy piggyback much of the way and Shelley still limping, their progress was slow. He wasn't surprised when she refused to rest, though. The lady had grit. He knew she wouldn't appreciate it if he voiced his thoughts aloud, so he kept them to himself.

Two hours later, they reached the spot where he'd parked the truck. The kind word for the 1982 Ford pickup he'd managed to acquire was *vin-*

tage, but the engine was sound, and it ran. That was all that mattered.

"How'd you get this?" she asked.

"I always keep some money tucked in my boot. For emergencies. I figured this qualified."

"You figured right."

Though the truck had definitely seen better days, it was sturdy and dry inside.

"Must be some emergency stash you keep in your boot."

"Enough," he said, then added, "when we were in country, we never knew when we were going to have to buy a truck or pay off an informant. It got to where we just started carrying cash. The universal language."

Finding a truck for under a thousand dollars hadn't been easy, but he'd managed. He'd been the unit's scavenger and had bought, bartered and traded whatever his guys had needed. It wasn't so different in the States.

"I don't know about you," Shelley said, "but I'm tired of being on the defensive."

"Hoo-yah. What are you proposing?"

"They're expecting us to zig."

A slow smile inched across his mouth. "And we're going to zag."

"Got it in one."

Shelley didn't object when he slid in behind the steering wheel. Once they reached the city, she gave him directions. He raised a brow as the surroundings grew more and more run-down. Houses and mom-and-pop stores were squeezed in between abandoned storefronts. Those few people on the street scurried to whatever destinations they had in mind.

"There," she said, pointing.

Caleb looked at the squat building fashioned from concrete blocks.

"What's this?"

"It's where people go when they have nowhere else."

SIX

Helping the homeless was Pastor Monson's mission in life. He had taken over the directorship of Helping Hands five years ago, attending to the physical and spiritual needs of the people who found their way there. He'd rejected the pastorship of a large church with its attendant prestige and salary in favor of serving society's forgotten people.

Since then, over five hundred had come and gone. Some had started new lives. Some had melted back in to the mean streets that were common to any large city. And some had simply disappeared.

When Shelley had asked him about why he did what he did, he'd said, "I know what it is to be lost. And I know what it is to be found. I decided to spend the rest of my life finding those lost ones."

Shelley introduced Caleb and Tommy and explained their situation.

"You're welcome here," the tall, distinguished-looking pastor said without hesitation.

"Thank you, Pastor. I knew we could count on you."

Caleb shifted Tommy in his arms, stuck out a hand. "Thank you for having us."

"Let me have the boy," Pastor Monson said. "He'll be well cared for here. Our residents look out for each other. When people have nothing, they tend to give everything."

Caleb placed Tommy into the older man's arms. "His parents were recently killed. He witnessed it. He hasn't spoken..." Caleb's voice broke. "I'm sorry."

"Don't be. You care about him. There's no shame in that."

For the first time in nearly a day, Shelley found she could smile. She had done the right thing, bringing Caleb and Tommy here. They needed rest from fear, from worry, and she needed time to regroup, to figure out a new game plan.

In the meantime, she hoped to do something to help Tommy. "After Tommy settles in, I'd like Cassie to look at him. She might find a way to reach him."

The pastor smiled. "If anyone can help him, it's Cassie." His smile grew. "And the Lord. We must never forget that He can perform miracles."

Shelley thought of the hours in the woods with Tommy. The Lord had sustained her through the darkness, just as He had sustained her through other trials. The thought gave her strength.

"Who's Cassie?" Caleb wanted to know.

"Cassie's a psychiatrist," the pastor said. "She volunteers here two days a week. She specializes in working with children."

Shelley reached for Caleb's hand. "Tommy's safe here."

The perfunctory nod he gave didn't fool her. Caleb wasn't one to accept someone else's word on something as important as his nephew's safety. She'd seen him scoping out the large room, his steely gaze sweeping the area with the expertise of someone accustomed to making critical deductions from what he observed. Windows, doors and stairways were evaluated in terms of escape should it prove necessary.

The pastor directed Shelley, Caleb and Tommy to the showers. "You'll be more comfortable when you've cleaned up," he said tactfully. "We've got some spare clothes you can change into when you're ready."

"Thank you."

Shelley nearly wept with gratitude for the soothing, hot spray of the shower. Mindful of the water bill and the shelter's limited funds, she kept her shower short, though she'd have gladly stayed there indefinitely. Though she still had a bit of a limp, the swelling in her ankle had gone down, and the pain was at least bearable.

She dressed in clean clothes borrowed from the donation bin and felt almost human. She found Caleb and Tommy similarly clean and dressed. She made time to call Sal, explain their situation and ask him to bring some clothes, two burner phones and another vehicle for them.

"Pastor, I can't thank you enough for putting us up for a few days," Shelley said as she and Caleb helped set the table. "If there's anything I can ever do…"

"As a matter of fact, there is," came the unexpected response. "Helping Hands is going to have to close its doors if we don't come up with some money soon."

She knew that the shelter operated on a shoestring, but she hadn't known how serious the situation was. "Some kind of fund-raiser. A benefit that would make money and make people aware of what you're doing here," she said, thinking aloud.

"Great," the pastor said heartily. "I know we're in good hands with you in charge."

"But I didn't…"

"Congratulations," Caleb said after the pastor went to greet some newcomers. "You just volunteered."

"I guess I did at that," she acknowledged with a wry chuckle.

With the other residents, they gathered for a

community meal of meatloaf, vegetables and mashed potatoes.

Caleb joined in with the mealtime conversation, participating in the lighthearted give-and-take, and she marveled at how good it was to see him like this, in ordinary circumstances, free from crisis mode. She didn't delude herself that the danger was over, but she was grateful for a respite from it all the same.

Following the meal, one of the volunteers settled Tommy in a circle with other children for story hour. Though he didn't participate, Tommy lost a bit of his blank-eyed stare.

Shelley watched as Caleb hovered, clearly reluctant to leave his nephew. "He'll be all right," she reassured him. "Like Pastor Monson said, the people here look out for each other. Especially the children."

"I like your Pastor Monson," Caleb said as he and Shelley helped with kitchen cleanup. Everyone pitched in to help, impressing him with their willingness to do what was necessary. While others cleared the tables, Shelley and Caleb started washing the dishes. The kitchen didn't boast a dishwasher. In fact, most of the appliances appeared to be of 1950s vintage.

"He's a good man. He used to be a cop."

Caleb lifted a brow. "Quite a career change. Cop to pastor to director of a homeless shelter."

"I used to think the same thing until he explained it to me. He said that he'd become a cop to help people, and he became a pastor for the same reason."

"Still."

"Yeah, still..." She looked thoughtful. "He said that he realized that when he was a cop, he was picking up the pieces after things had already gone horribly wrong."

"And he became a pastor to keep things from going wrong in the first place." It made sense, though Caleb knew it wasn't as simple as that.

"Something like that."

"Do you know him well?" he asked curiously.

"I met him shortly after I moved to Atlanta. He helped me out on a case. I like his way of looking at the world."

"And what's that?" Caleb realized he really wanted to know.

"That each of us, no matter who we are in life, can make a difference."

He narrowed his eyes. "Is that why you do what you do? To make a difference?"

"I like to think I am," she said softly, at last. "Helping people who are in trouble. Sometimes I succeed. Sometimes I don't. But at least I know I've tried."

He wasn't surprised at her answer. He was beginning to realize that Shelley Rabb was a special kind of woman. A warrior. A believer. She was all those things, and more.

"For what it's worth, you're making a difference to me. To Tommy." He hesitated. "Why is that so important to you? Making a difference."

She didn't answer right away, and he wondered if he'd gone too far, asking something so personal. She stilled, as though searching her heart as to how much she should reveal, how much she *wanted* to reveal.

As a man who guarded his own privacy, he understood. Giving away too much of one's self left a person vulnerable. That was something Caleb had promised himself he'd never be. It had taken Michael's death to remind him that he was as vulnerable as the next guy.

"I don't have many memories of my mother," Shelley said in a barely audible voice. "But when I think about how she deserted Jake and me, I knew I didn't want to be like her, caring only about myself. I wanted to do something to help others, which is why I became a cop and then an agent. When that ended, I wanted to use my training. Opening a security/protection firm seemed the answer."

That wasn't all of it.

Shelley recalled the sleepless nights she'd spent on her knees, begging the Lord for guidance after she'd left the Service. The answer she'd received, to start her own business, had strengthened her relationship with God in ways she'd never expected. As she helped her clients, people who often had no one else on their side, she began to more fully understand God's desire to help His children.

"You made your choices count," Caleb said, drawing her back to the present.

"Like you."

"I tried," he said gruffly. "Right now, I'm feeling like I made the wrong ones."

"No. You did what was right at the time."

"About that benefit... I might be able to help," Caleb said unexpectedly.

She looked at him in surprise. That was the last thing she'd expected. What did an army Delta know about throwing a benefit? Apparently he guessed at her thoughts, for he smiled. "Some of the guys' wives are big on fund-raising for good causes. I know they'd like to help with Helping Hands."

Caleb was a contradiction. He was both a tough-as-nails soldier and a deeply compassionate man who wanted to help a bunch of people he'd barely met. There were lines around his eyes, crow's feet etched more deeply than a civilian's. Carrying a weapon, defending his country against those determined to destroy it, did that to a person. She'd seen it in Jake and others.

Those lines were visible. But what of those

that festered inside? Though not visible, they ran deep. She knew Caleb wouldn't want to hear that, so she focused on the benefit.

"That'd be great. The shelter is always short of funds. There's so much that the residents need. The pastor does his best, but it's not easy." She sighed. "People look at anyone who's homeless and then look away. No one wants to admit that there are real people who fall through the cracks every day, many of them children. They deserve better."

"You're right. They do. Between the two of us, we'll make it happen."

Shelley's heart lifted at the promise in his voice. He'd just met the pastor and a few of the residents, but he wanted to help.

Unbidden, a picture of Caleb in evening attire appeared in her mind, and suddenly there was nothing she wanted more at that moment than to see him in a dapper tux. He'd look good in anything, but in a tux...he'd be heart-stopping.

She pushed the tantalizing image from her mind. Protecting Tommy and finding Michael's killers were the only things Caleb wanted from her. Once that was done, he'd go back to Delta, and she...well, she had a life here.

He rubbed a hand over his jaw, drawing her attention to the rugged lines of his face. Long and lean, the hard edge of the soldier was on his face. He slumped forward in his chair. Worry dulled his eyes, not even the laser-sharp blue gaze able to penetrate them.

One hand closed into a fist, as though he had to do something and didn't know what. *What must it take for a man accustomed to action to be forced to wait?* she mused.

Her fingers itched to soothe the lines of stress from his face, but she kept her hands at her sides.

For more than a few reasons, Caleb Judd intrigued her. She'd tried analyzing why. He was not the first attractive man she'd ever met. Her work in the DC Police Department, then in the Service, had put her in the vicinity of a number of strong, handsome men, but none had affected her as Caleb did. Not even Jeffrey, whom she'd once thought might be *the one.*

Her admiration for Caleb ratcheted up another notch as she thought of how he kept himself focused, despite his worry.

"How'd you and the pastor meet?"

"I took a job protecting the daughter of an oil tycoon. There'd been some threats, toward him and his family. He was afraid of kidnapping and came to me."

Caleb nodded, encouraging her to continue with the story.

"The daughter was an only child and beyond spoiled. Didn't want to follow the rules, even when it was for her own safety. Finally I got fed up. I took her to the shelter, let her see how those who weren't as fortunate as she was lived. The people here showed the girl just how rough things could be. They gave her an eye-opener I don't think she'll ever forget.

"Pastor Monson and I have been friends ever since." Shelley's voice turned admiring. "He's done more for the people of this city than the mayor and all the so-called city fathers combined."

Caleb raised a brow. "Sounds like you don't have much use for politicians."

"I spent eight years in Washington," Shelley said, flashing a droll smile. "There's nothing a politician could do that would surprise me. Not anymore."

"We're on the same page there. Ask any soldier what he thinks of politicians. They come in, expect to be treated like big shots, then take time and resources away from doing the job."

"Jake's told me stories."

"Believe them. And more. The politicians have their own agenda. Rarely does it match that of the men and women in the trenches." He gave her a curious look. "What happened to the oil tycoon's daughter?"

"She straightened herself out. Last I heard she was going to college and volunteering at a homeless shelter in her spare time." Shelley's smile widened. "Her father gave me a bonus. He said she was a changed person."

"You made a difference."

Shelley shook her head. "Not me. It was Pastor Monson and the people here."

"It's personal for you, isn't it? Helping here."

His insight took her by surprise. "You could say that."

"Meaning…?"

She hesitated. Before she could talk herself out of it, she started talking. "I went through the typical teenage rebellion. I gave Jake plenty of grief, pushing him away, when all he was trying to do was to take care of me. Then I did something really dumb…" Her voice faltered, but then she dragged in a deep breath and plowed on. "I ran away and ended up in a house with a bunch of other kids. When some of them started boosting cars, I objected."

Caleb didn't say anything, only waited.

"One of the boys tied me up in a chair, left me in the basement. I screamed until I was hoarse." She cleared her throat, relieved to get that part out. The memory of that time, the basement alive with the sound of rats scurrying across the floor, still caused her to tremble inside. That hadn't been the first time she'd been locked in a dark place and it had reinforced her fear. "I don't know if I'd ever have gotten out of there, except the cops raided the place and found me. They called Jake, who read me the riot act."

It felt right when Caleb enveloped her hand between his own. "I'm glad you told me."

So was she.

"Jake never stopped loving me, no matter what I did or said. I owe him."

"He wouldn't want that."

"No. But it's the truth." From that time on, she'd searched for the truth. Truth didn't let you down, like some people did. And wasn't that what she was doing now, searching for the truth about what happened to Tommy's parents?

Whatever else she and Caleb found, they would uncover the truth. That was a promise she made to herself with every job she undertook. Sometimes that truth took her to unwanted places, but truth always came out in the end.

"Jake told me that if I were going to make something of myself, I needed to let go of the past and to move forward. I guess that's what I've been trying to do ever since. Move forward."

"I'd say that you more than made something of yourself," Caleb murmured and tucked a stray strand of hair behind her ear.

The sweetness of the gesture touched something deep inside of her.

As she talked, Shelley fought against her reaction to Caleb Judd's raw brand of masculinity. It annoyed her that she was thinking of him rather than focusing on the job. She studied him as she would a client, saw the taut line of muscle and bone around his jaw.

The tension of wondering when and where the next threat was coming had clearly taken a toll on him, gnawing away at his insides.

Today, his blue eyes were paler than usual, as though worry had leached the color from them, and his cheeks were sunken and hollow. Likewise, his mouth tightened into a thin, hard line as though each breath were a stab to his heart. She suspected that any physical wound he'd suffered would never compare to the pain he was enduring now.

A lump rose to Shelley's throat. She would have felt the same if she'd lost Jake. He was her touchstone, her mainstay in a world that too often failed to make sense. What must it have cost Caleb to lose both his brothers?

Despite the despair that cast his face into harsh shadows, he was an attractive man. Not traditionally handsome, she thought. His face was too rugged, too lived-in for that, but there was something undeniably compelling about him.

Shaken by the turn of her thoughts, she gave herself a mental shake and remembered she had a strict no-involvement policy with clients. The feelings Caleb awakened in her threatened the wall of professionalism she'd built around herself. That spelled disaster, in more ways than one.

Look at what had happened with Jeffrey when she'd given in to the attraction for a coworker.

So why then did she want to throw out the rule book when it came to Caleb?

Mentally flicking a switch, she steered away from the emotional minefield of her past and refocused on the present. When she surfaced from her thoughts, she realized that Caleb's gaze rested on her with unmistakable warmth. Just as quickly, it was banked.

He rolled his shoulders, and she saw the weariness in his eyes as he rubbed the back of his neck.

Part of her job was to assess the client's state of mind. It didn't take much reasoning to figure out that Caleb was beating himself up over his brother and sister-in-law's deaths. Again.

She longed to smooth her hand over his forehead, to wipe away the trenches there, but she kept her hands to herself. "Give it a rest, Judd."

"I should have been there for Michael and his family." The twisting of his lips held more than a hint of bitterness.

"You can't do anything for Michael and Grace now. They're in God's hands. But you're here for their son. You're standing by Tommy. That's what family does." Though she hadn't had loving parents, she'd had Jake, who had always done his best by her.

"Jake was my family. After that, the Metro

PD and then the Service. We are what we make ourselves," she said. "What you've made of yourself says a lot about you. The kind of man you are. The kind who stands up for those who can't stand up for themselves."

She'd learned enough about Caleb to realize that he would always expect more from himself than he did anyone else. She took her time in framing the next question. "What happened between you and Michael?"

"On my last leave home, I told him he ought to withdraw from the case, that it was too dangerous."

Shelley couldn't help the grin that tugged at her mouth. "If he's anything like you, I can imagine how that went over."

He smiled sheepishly back at her. "He told me to stop playing big brother and to mind my own business. We both said some things we shouldn't have but were too stubborn to take back."

"And?"

"And we didn't talk after that." His lips twisted. "We didn't have any communication at all. Except for the text. It came three days before...it happened."

"A text?"

"It didn't make much sense. Only three words. *Bear with me.*"

"'Bear with me'?"

"I tried to figure it out, but all I could come up with was that he was trying to apologize."

"Not much of an apology."

A shrug. "Michael and I weren't much on saying we're sorry. Especially to each other..." She waited patiently for him to continue.

"I should have known that Michael was in over his head. Maybe I did and ignored it. I had to go off and play soldier." Caleb pinched the bridge of his nose. "What if he never knew how much I loved him?"

"Don't do this to yourself. You deserve better. So do Michael and Grace and Tommy."

Caleb was silent for long moments. "Thank you."

Sincerely baffled, she asked, "For what?"

"For taking the time to make me remember. I was there for Michael. As much as I could be."

She squeezed his hand.

"Seeing him and Grace together, just watching them look at each other, it was almost like seeing God." A brief smile flickered across Caleb's mouth. "I know. That sounds really over-the-top, doesn't it? Comparing that to seeing the Lord. But that's how it was."

Though he still looked tough and hard, his voice had softened, and then she got it. He was embarrassed. The big bad Delta didn't want her to witness the momentary vulnerability.

She wanted to wrap her arms around him, to

tell him that he had no reason to be embarrassed in front of her. Because she knew. She felt the same way about seeing Jake and Dani together.

But she didn't. Didn't wrap her arms around his neck. Didn't tell him. Didn't do anything. Because she didn't know how.

Caleb pressed the heels of his hands to his eyes. When he removed his hands, his expression was unbelievably bleak, and she sensed he was going to tell her something important.

"Michael and I had a younger brother. Ethan."

She nodded. "The newspaper clipping said he drowned."

Caleb didn't so much nod as grimace. "He died when he was only a toddler. My fault."

"How old were you?"

"Six."

"You were a baby yourself." But Caleb wasn't listening, his eyes unfocused as though he were looking for something that wasn't there. "Our mother told me to watch Michael and Ethan while she answered the phone. Ethan fell in the pool. He drowned before I could get to him." The staccato sentences delivered in a matter-of-fact tone told their own story.

Shelley struggled to suppress her gasp. "It wasn't your fault."

"Try telling that to my mother."

"She blamed you?"

Caleb's laugh held not a trace of humor. "You

could say that. She never said a kind word to me after that day. In fact, she did her best to avoid talking to me at all. We haven't seen each other since the day I graduated from high school."

Shelley's heart clutched. Resentment splashed over her. Not at Caleb, but at the mother who placed that kind of burden on a six-year-old child. Her outrage pushed her out of the chair to pace back and forth, arms crossed tightly over her chest.

She stopped in front of him. "You can't believe that you were at fault. You're too smart for that."

The truth lay in his eyes, on his face. Raw. Painful. So much so that she wanted to wipe away the self-loathing she saw there.

"Rationally, I knew I wasn't to blame," he said, voice hollow. "But it didn't matter."

"What about your father?"

"My old man did the best he could, but he never could stand up to my mother. He died the year before I graduated," Caleb added, almost as an afterthought.

"And you and Michael?"

"We took care of ourselves for the most part. We used to joke that it was us against the world." The agony radiating in his voice called to her.

Her heart broke a little with every word, but she was powerless to take away his pain. Desperately, she searched for something to put things back on a professional basis.

"The clipping you got at the Kruises' guest-house," Shelley said. "It had to have been sent by someone who knew about Ethan, how he died."

"I've been thinking about that," Caleb said, the expression in his eyes telling her that he knew what she was doing and was grateful for it. "I don't go around telling people about it. In fact, you're the only person I've talked to about it in years."

"What about Michael? Would he have told someone?"

"I don't know." Caleb shoved a hand through his hair. "He and I never talked about it much. Michael was too young to remember and I…"

"Someone had to know," she said quietly. "Had to know how to use it against you."

They'd miscalculated, though, she thought. It hadn't made him turn tail and run. On the contrary, it made him more determined than ever to find the truth.

"Ethan died more than a quarter of a century ago," he bit out.

"It's a matter of public record. Anyone could have looked it up. Someone knew what it would do to you.

"My people are working with the police on the envelope and the clipping. So far, there's nothing. No fingerprints. Which we expected. There might be DNA trace, but that takes time." She grimaced. "Unlike on TV, DNA can't be processed in forty-seven minutes."

She leaned closer, stopped. The anguish on his face gutted her. But what did *she* know about giving comfort? Her efforts at helping Jake during the dark nightmares that had plagued him had proven how little she knew. There'd been no mother to give her an example of feminine caring.

No, giving solace wasn't her finest skill. She could strip down an AK-47 in under a minute, disarm a man twice her size using only her bare hands and make a not-too-shabby showing in a triathlon. She could do all that and more, but she didn't know how to offer comfort.

Never had she felt that lack so keenly as she did now. Should she try to say something? Or should she keep her mouth shut? What if she said the wrong thing? What if she made things worse? What if...

She prayed for the right words—any words. Abruptly the realization struck her that words weren't what Caleb needed. Not now. Without giving herself time to talk herself out of it, she went to him, wrapped her arms around him.

And held him.

Caleb didn't try to pull away as she'd feared. Instead, he closed his arms around her. How long they stayed that way, she didn't know. If anyone saw them, they were tactful enough not to interrupt.

"Thank you," he said at last. "Thank you."

With evening, the shelter had quieted. The temperature had mercifully dropped. Only in the high eighties now, Shelley reflected wryly, with matching humidity.

Shelley shifted on the sleeping cot and swiped a hand across her forehead which was wicking off sweat. Her body begged for sleep, but her mind refused to settle. It wasn't the heat, or even the humidity, that was making her feel out of sorts.

She was feeling out of her depth. Her specialty lay in providing security for corporate tycoons. Now she was developing real feelings for the uncle of the pint-size witness she was assigned to protect. The steady rhythm of rain on the cheap tin roof should have soothed her. It didn't.

As much as possible, families were kept together at the shelter. Though she wasn't family to Caleb or Tommy, Pastor Monson had arranged for her to take a cot near them.

Even surrounded by people she'd come to know—both volunteers and residents—she was grateful for the heaviness of her weapon at her side. The threats to Tommy and Caleb hadn't ended.

As per usual at the end of the day, she asked

for the Lord's blessing on her efforts in safe-guarding her clients. Praying for her clients was a matter of course, but tonight's prayer was more than that. The words came straight from her heart and soul, a pleading for the Lord's mercy upon both Tommy and Caleb.

In the short time she'd known him, Tommy had retreated further and further into himself, as if the outside world was too painful to engage. Though she had no experience with children, no idea of what they needed, she understood enough to know that he was losing himself in a private world of his own making. Her heart ached for him.

Caleb tugged at her heart, as well. Guilt and grief and anguish were eating at him, chewing him up and spitting him out. She longed to ease his suffering, to succor the man beneath the hard-edged Delta exterior.

Complicating matters were her growing feelings for him. A casual glance from him had the power to make her pulse race. An accidental touch made her skin tingle.

More than her physical attraction to him, though, were her feelings for the man himself. He was a warrior; at the same time, he was a protector, an honorable man with a strong sense of right and wrong.

He was the kind of man she'd dreamed of, a man who would love a woman and love the Lord with his whole being. Duty was as important to him as it was to her. Right now, hers lay in keeping him and Tommy out of harm's way.

Her focus needed to be there, not on her feelings for the uncle. She'd failed the Service, failed her fallen comrade, failed herself. She couldn't, wouldn't, fail Caleb and Tommy. She summoned every bit of resolve she had and forced her traitorous emotions from her mind, determined to sleep.

Exhaustion hovered. Shelley nearly surrendered to its lure when a tortured cry pulled her from it.

SEVEN

It was three in the morning when Caleb found himself in the mountains of Afghanistan in the midst of an ambush, one that he and his men lost every time. Automatic weapon fire punched through the night, with its staccato tat-tat-tat-tat.

His unit had been assigned to take out a high-value target. It had been a setup, but, by the time they realized that, it had been too late.

Cries ripped through the night as the enemy descended upon the small unit of men. Outnumbered five to one, they fought valiantly, but they couldn't defeat the superior forces.

"No. No!" Caleb screamed out as Tinks went down. Tinks, who had a perpetual grin on his face and a heart big enough to care about the forgotten children who moved like shadows through a land ravaged by war. Tinks, who had pulled Caleb from a burning jeep just before it exploded.

Caleb made to go to his fallen buddy when

strong hands pulled him back, shook him. "He's gone, Judd. We need you alive if we're gonna make it out of here."

That was Tin-Man, so named because he could quote dialogue from *The Wizard of Oz* forward and backward. "Get your head in the game or we're all dead."

It had worked. Caleb had done what he'd been trained to do. He'd set his sights on the enemy and did the job, blanking his mind to the blood spilled, blood on both sides. Automatically, his mind calculated wind direction and distance with each bullet he fired. Ammunition was at a premium, and he needed to make every shot count.

In the end, three men had died. Caleb had walked away with a medal he neither wanted nor deserved. What was a piece of metal when compared to the lives of friends?

"Caleb. Caleb." A soft voice penetrated the pain-infused nightmare.

He jerked awake, instantly alert and ready for action, jaw set, hands fisted. The combat stance was as natural as breathing.

Ironically, it was the humidity, pressing in from all sides, that brought him back to the here and now. The Stand had never known the wet heaviness in the air that defied the puny attempts of the shelter's single air-conditioning unit. He took a long breath in an effort to calm the racing of his heart. Another.

Slowly, his thoughts settled as reality returned. Michael. Grace. Tommy.

There was no sense in denying that he hadn't been startled by Shelley's touch. It was a wonder he hadn't flattened her, a leftover from his training.

Caleb sank his face into his hands. Grief over the botched mission still managed to ambush him, sneaking up when it was least expected and clawing at his heart until he felt he'd surely bleed to death from it. Guilt sharpened its teeth on him that he had escaped unscathed while others had died. If he'd acted faster, if he'd been smarter, if…

"Sorry," Shelley said and took a cautious step back. "I didn't mean to spook you."

"I'm the one who's sorry," he rasped, looking at his raised hands, hands that had taken lives, ready to strike, to inflict pain. Slowly, he unclenched his fingers, one by one, at the same time, unclenching the tightening in his chest. "If I'd hurt you…" He couldn't finish the thought. The idea that he might have injured Shelley sent a chill spiraling down his spine.

"You didn't." Her smile was easy. "Hey," she said when he didn't return it. "I'm no hothouse flower. I've seen my share of rough duty." Her voice was measured and even, in direct contrast to his own guttural, emotion-laden tones.

"Not from me you haven't." He was still

shocked by what he'd almost done. Another second and he would have had her pinned to the floor, hand at her throat. He ran his tongue over his teeth; at the same time, he tried to rub the grit from his eyes.

Shelley gestured to the living area.

With a glance at the sleeping Tommy, Caleb nodded.

Crowded with secondhand furniture, the common room was shabby with its faux-wood paneling and green shag carpet from decades ago. But the overstuffed sofas appeared inviting and promised comfort.

Away from those who were sleeping, Shelley curled her hands around his arms. Though she barely came to his shoulders, her gentle touch exuded strength. "Want to talk about it?"

"When I'm tired, the nightmares come back."

"It's all right."

But it wasn't. When he'd been in country, he had gone for days with little or no sleep, his body trained to withstand sleep deprivation, hunger and all manner of hardship. He'd handled it all without breaking stride. Ever since learning of Michael and Grace's deaths, though, he felt as if he'd been running on empty.

He and Shelley sat on an overstuffed orange sofa that looked like a misshapen pumpkin.

"It would be strange if you weren't tired," she said. "Ever since we met, we've been dodging bullets and playing hide-and-seek with people who want you dead."

"Deltas don't get tired." He blurted the words without thinking. Deltas plowed through mud and muck and all manner of things that would send a civilian running in the opposite direction. Tired? It wasn't an option.

She made a rude sound at that.

The mission was pain fresh in his mind, his own failures an open wound that had scabbed over but had never healed. The nightmare was a too-common occurrence, one he'd done his best to eradicate, and, when that didn't work, to ignore.

No Delta wanted to be considered weak. A muttered "Man up" was as close as they got to offering comfort to each other in the alpha male society of special ops.

"One thing I've learned is not to look back. Learn from the past, sure, but don't dwell on it. Keep moving forward." Giving in to the nightmare meant he hadn't moved forward. And it shamed him.

"Is that what you did when you were in Delta? Keep moving forward?"

"I had to. It was that or die. Even when it seemed hopeless, I kept moving forward. An inch at a time. Another. There was a time..." He shook his head, a futile attempt to wipe away the memory. "I wasn't sure we'd make it. Somehow we held on until help arrived. There are some things a man doesn't forget."

He drew in her scent, fresh peaches with vanilla lapping right underneath. Her shampoo, he guessed. How long had it been since he'd actually noticed how a woman smelled?

He shoved that aside. Right now, his focus had to be on Tommy.

"He's all right," Shelley said, apparently guessing at Caleb's thoughts.

Caleb exhaled a shaky breath. Of course he knew Tommy was all right, but he couldn't turn off the worry.

At the same time, he basked in the knowledge that Shelley was on his side. Her presence was comforting, like being cocooned in a down sleeping bag in the mountains. He'd felt so cold, so alone, but with Shelley, the loneliness was fading.

Despite the constant worry and fear, he felt a measure of peace.

The contradiction of fear and peace didn't seem so strange when he realized that he could no longer bury his feelings as he'd done in Delta. He was no longer the same man he'd been.

9/11 had forever changed him, as it had so many. When the planes had hit the Twin Towers, he'd been a college student, coasting through school and life, little more on his mind than making it through the next physics test and taking his girl out for dinner and a movie.

Shallow didn't begin to describe him. That infamous day had triggered something within him. He'd finished out the semester and, without talking with anyone, had enlisted.

"The Deltas made me," he said. "They took a boy and turned him into a man." He paused. "I almost didn't make it."

He took a moment, remembering. The training had been grueling, but he'd thrived in the disciplined atmosphere and the sense of brotherhood he'd found. He volunteered for the most dangerous missions and took intense satisfaction in fighting America's enemies, believing he was making a difference.

"But you did," Shelley said, drawing him back to the present.

"Yeah. I did. Thanks to God and to some friends who wouldn't let me quit. It was the best thing that could have happened to me." The smile that had flirted with the corners of his mouth disappeared abruptly. He'd been itching to go, to fight in a war on the other side of the world, and had left his brother behind, his brother who was fighting his own kind of war.

Now they were all paying the price for his self-absorption.

He made himself take a calming breath, then another. His hands were shaking, his stomach muscles in a tight grip, acid churning. Why had going halfway around the world to fight a war that no one was ever going to win seemed so important?

He looked up to find Shelley staring at him, her soft gray eyes shimmering with empathy and compassion. Their gazes met and held, a silent understanding passing between them.

Something was going on between him and Shelley, something beyond the job. Relationships, outside of those with his family and a few friends, were out of his realm and he realized he was navigating his way through uncharted territory.

"Shelley, I—"

"Shh," she said softly. "It's okay."

The raw, jagged emotions he felt for her were at odds with the sense of peace he experienced in her presence. How could she inspire both? From the first, he'd sensed that the lady was a contradiction. It shouldn't surprise him that the feelings she roused within him would be equally contradictory.

Without his knowing quite how it happened, he found himself telling Shelley about the mission in Afghanistan, the ambush, the horror of watching friends die.

"In the end, Little Birds got us out."

"Little Birds?"

"Small helicopters. MD530s."

Though they lacked the presence of the much larger Bell 412 choppers, the Little Birds got the job done. With a speed of one hundred and twenty knots, they were fast, agile and could carry four men inside with four more riding on the skids. He had ridden the Little Birds into some pretty hairy situations, and they had always come through.

"I should have been smarter," he concluded the story. "I should have known we were outnumbered, but I had my orders. Because I didn't listen to my gut, three men died."

With four other Deltas, he'd returned to the site to bring back the bodies of his fallen comrades before the enemy could take them and desecrate them.

"Do you think those men would want you blaming yourself?"

"It doesn't matter. I blame myself." Caleb rolled his shoulders in a futile attempt to relieve the knots that had taken up residence there.

"Is that what they would want? What *you* would want if the positions were reversed?"

He didn't have to think about it. "No."

"Then forgive yourself."

"It's not that easy," he croaked.

"Do you believe that God forgives you?"

Her question startled him. What did that have to do with the mission? "Of course…" Did he? Did he truly believe that God forgave him?

"The Lord is there for you. All you have to do is ask Him. His forgiveness is there for all of us. He has already paid for our sins, our weaknesses, our sorrows, our tears." She leaned closer, lifting her gaze to his. "You blamed yourself for your men's death and now for Michael's death. Hand it over to the Lord. Let Him shoulder the burden. He's the only One who can."

Caleb wanted to believe her. Was it really that simple?

Tears leaked from his eyes, made their way down his cheeks. He thumbed them away, then stared in amazement at the glistening drops.

Caleb didn't cry. *Ever.* He hadn't shed a tear when men around him lay dying on the battlefield. Nor had he cried when he'd taken the lives of enemies. Among his buddies, he had the reputation of never divulging his thoughts or feelings. Friends and enemies alike claimed that he didn't blink an eye, no matter how dire the situation.

He hadn't allowed himself to feel grief when buddies died. And he hadn't allowed himself to feel anger when he went into combat. Feelings made you weak, and weakness made you fail. It was that simple.

There'd been times when he'd willed the tears to come, if for no other reason than to give relief to the pressure in his eyes. His soul. But the tears had refused to bleed through his eyes. As for his soul, apparently it was too parched to give up anything, much less the needed moisture for tears.

Caleb drew in a deep, bracing breath, let it out slowly. His life, that of his comrades, depended upon his being in control. Always. So what was he doing crying like a baby now, in front of a woman he'd known only a handful of days?

That wasn't him. But, then, nothing was like him right now. He barely recognized himself. How could he?

Everything he thought he knew, everything he thought he was, had been stripped away with Michael's death. It had taken his brother being murdered to pierce his shell and make him as vulnerable as the next guy.

How could he expect things to be the same? And now…now he was guardian to Michael's son. Would he make a mess of that just as he seemed to have done with everything else? Ruthlessly, he locked the images away.

He knew Shelley was watching him, her eyes full of sympathy. He should tell her to go, to let him grieve alone. To his surprise, though, he discovered he didn't want to be alone.

She laid her hand on his, folded her fingers around his own.

Her touch sparked unexpected feelings through him, and, without thinking, he touched his lips to hers. The kiss lasted less than a minute, but it carried a powerful punch. Reluctantly, he pulled away.

Caleb called himself all sorts of a fool. What had he been thinking, kissing her that way? He wasn't given to impulsive gestures, much less kissing a woman he barely knew. Especially there, in the shelter.

As much as he admired Shelley, he couldn't afford to have feelings for her. Even if he were free to pursue a relationship, which he wasn't, Shelley wasn't the right woman for him. She'd admitted that she had no experience with children, and was, in fact, afraid of them.

Tommy was part of Caleb's life now. Permanently. When—*if*—he found a woman he could love, she needed to be able to accept Tommy.

That settled, he told himself he felt better.

He chalked up the kiss to worry and exhaustion and tried not to think about Shelley's sweet, infectious smile. The smattering of freckles across her nose. How her soft, full lips fit perfectly against his…

He frowned, frustrated with himself for spending even a moment ruminating about a woman who meant nothing to him outside of helping him protect Tommy and finding the lowlifes who murdered his brother.

Liar.

* * *

Shelley hadn't thought it was possible for her heart to beat any faster.

The kiss startled her. Captivated her. Reminded her how easily she could come to care about Caleb, not just as a client but as a man.

She gathered her composure. Or what was left of it.

"I'm sorry." Caleb's voice sounded as frayed as her emotions.

Whatever had prompted the embrace was gone, and in its place was an awkwardness on his part that made her cringe.

"Don't. Just...don't." She resisted burying her face in her hands. Was there anything worse than having a man kiss her and then apologize?

It was obvious Caleb regretted the lip-lock. She wasn't about to make more of it than it was. Despite that resolve, her thoughts were scrambled to the point that she struggled to remember her own name.

"You've heard all about my dysfunctional family," he said thickly. "What about you? Any skeletons in your family closet?"

She understood what Caleb was asking. He'd shared a painful part of his past with her and was now challenging her to do the same.

"Jake may have told you that our father took off before I was born," she said.

"He said something about it."

"Did he say anything about our mother?" Her voice caught on the last word.

"Just that she didn't stick around long."

"That's one way of putting it." She paused, wondering how much she wanted to share, how much she *should* share. "My mother never wanted me. She made that plain from the first. Jake was the one who made sure I had food in my belly, clothes on my back, and went to school.

"But he wasn't there all the time. He had a part-time job delivering papers, trying to make enough money to buy a few groceries. Whenever she wanted to go out and Jake wasn't around to watch me, she'd lock me in the storage unit of the apartment building.

"I still can't stand dark places." Her laugh was self-deprecating. "Pretty pathetic, huh? A grown woman who gets the heebie-jeebies in the dark. When Jake found out about it, he threatened to call social services. I guess that's when *mommy dearest* decided she'd had enough." A shudder coursed through her at the memory of being imprisoned in the darkness. The fear had been reinforced years later when the boys had locked her in the basement. "I always wondered if there were a part of her in me. That I'd do to another kid what she did to me."

Caleb had remained silent during the recitation. "Your mother sounds like a real piece of work."

She warmed at the outrage in his voice. At the same time, she cringed at the compassion she read in his eyes. "Save your sympathy. And your pity," she said, her voice light, though her knuckles whitened, as though trying to repress unwanted memories. "I told you so that you'd know why I keep my distance from Tommy. If there's any part of that woman in me... I can't risk hurting a child."

"You're not like her."

"How do you know? We've known each other, what—less than two days? You don't know what I'm capable of. Cruelty is in my blood." She said it with cool acceptance, though the idea that she might be like her mother filled her with horror. Then she looked away.

Caleb reached out to gently cup her cheek and turned her face toward his. "That's where you're wrong. You put yourself on the line for Tommy and me over and over. That tells me a lot."

For years after her mother abandoned Shelley and Jake, Shelley had searched the mail, looking for a card, a letter, something to let her know that her mother still thought of her. She'd run to answer the phone whenever it rang, certain that this would be *the* call—the one that assured her that her mother loved her, that she'd had no choice in leaving, that she would return someday and make everything right.

But it had never come.

She'd had Jake, and that had been enough. He had raised her to stand on her own. He had given her that, perhaps even then accepting he might not always be around. When she'd been old enough to take care of herself, he'd enlisted in the army.

"I need to do my part," he'd said when she'd asked why. "We all need to do our part."

It was that, she supposed, that had prompted her to put in her papers to enter the police academy. From there, it hadn't been a huge jump to make the switch to the Service.

It was a good life, but sometimes, like now, she wished she didn't feel so awkward in the art of giving and receiving comfort.

Sweeping her gaze over Caleb's tired, grief-stricken face, her stomach churned. Even though he had tried to shift the focus to her, she knew deep down inside he needed something. *Someone*. And she was the only one there.

Silently, she prayed that she could give him what he needed, that, if only for this moment, she could be enough. Her palms grew wet, her breathing ragged. She'd faced down armed assailants with far less anxiety than wondering what to do for this grieving man.

She knelt beside him, wrapped her arms around him and held tight. Together, they rocked back and forth, she doing her best to absorb his pain, to take it inside of her.

Please, Lord, give me the wisdom to help Caleb. He's hurting, and I don't know what to do.

And then it came. She could be there for him. Even if she didn't have the right words, she could listen and try to understand.

It's okay to let go, she wanted to tell Caleb. *You don't need to be a brave warrior all the time.* Instinctively, she knew he would reject those words, so she said the only thing she could. "It's all right." She murmured the words over and over, praying they would reach him, praying she could make it so.

Tentatively, she touched his hand and tenderness flowed between them. Did he feel it, as well? She didn't know.

She had to concentrate to hear his next words, so low was his voice.

"It will never be all right again…my fault. I wasn't there for him when he needed me." He spoke in a raspy whisper, as though each word were chiseled from a chunk of ice. His voice was raw with pain, his expression tormented, his features edged with failure and despair.

She ached for him. Once again, prayed for the right words. "You're here now. You're here for Michael's son," she repeated firmly. "Make it count."

The silence was loud enough to block out everything else, including the beating of her own heart, and she thought he was going to ignore what she'd said. A look of gratitude flickered across his face.

"Thank you."

That wasn't what she'd expected, but, then nothing about Caleb Judd was what she'd expected.

"It's the truth." And it was. Caleb was here now. He was doing everything in his power to protect Tommy.

His quick, derisive snort caused a painful jab, but she was determined to get through to him.

Sounds from the sleeping areas reminded her that they weren't alone. Anyone could enter the living area at any time. "It's morning," she said in surprise, wondering where the night had gone.

The next hour was spent seeing to Tommy, making sure he had something to eat and then settling him with a group of children in the reading and play group the mothers at the shelter held every morning.

When she volunteered her and Caleb's services to do the breakfast cleanup, Pastor Monson had given her a shrewd look. "Of course. You'll have the kitchen to yourselves."

Not much slipped by the man, Shelley reflected. Somehow he knew something was going on between her and Caleb, and he was giving them the time and space to work it out.

She set to work, stacking the dishes and then

running hot, soapy water. "I wash, you dry," she said.

Caleb picked up a dish towel.

"You're pretty good at that," she mused as they worked their way through the piles and piles of dirty dishes.

"You know the old saying about the army running on its stomach?" At her nod, he drawled, "It goes double for Delta. I've washed and dried enough dishes, peeled enough potatoes and made enough high-octane coffee to open my own restaurant."

The homey task was at odds with the tension sheening the air around them.

When the cleanup was finally done, she pulled out two kitchen chairs, took one and gestured to the other.

Clearly unable to bear standing still, Caleb ignored it and paced back and forth, his long strides eating up the limited space. She saw his chest heave as he struggled to breathe and knew all too well how easy it was to lose one's self when the anguish and grief grew too great. Her heart thumped along with his as she willed him to take the next breath. The next. And the next.

He would stew in his worry if she didn't intercede.

"You're a good man, Caleb Judd. Stop beating yourself up and accept it."

"A good man would have been here for his brother and his family."

So they were back to that again. She sighed.

"Don't make me out to be some kind of dime-store hero," he said, the roughness of his words the only defense.

A shadow moved into his eyes, and she knew he was thinking about Michael and Grace and Tommy.

"I know," she said softly. "Losing people we love hurts. It's part of caring." She reached out to him. "And we'll make sure that Tommy gets the help he needs."

She scarcely noticed her use of the word *we*. It seemed only natural that she would help Tommy in any way she could, even after the job was finished. She hitched her chin toward a vinyl-covered chair next to her.

He lowered his big, muscular frame into it.

The ease with which she'd included herself in helping Tommy signaled a shift in their relationship. Awareness flickered between them, stretching the moment until she mentally shook her head at herself.

Abruptly, Caleb laughed, a strangled sound. "I can't keep thinking about Tommy. About what happens if we don't find whoever's after him."

His voice cracked, and something cracked inside her at that single sign of emotion. Now that he'd given voice to the fear, she figured he was about five seconds from shutting down completely, and if he did that, she was afraid there might not be another window inside him.

"We'll find out who murdered your brother and his wife." She had no right to make that kind of promise, had, in fact, told herself that she couldn't make any promises, but she was unable to help herself.

Caleb was desperate to believe her. She saw it in his eyes, in the tightening of his mouth. But he knew, as well as she did, that the likelihood of finding the murderers decreased with every day that went by.

"Sorry about last night, almost attacking you and all." His voice was gruff. "Chalk it up to too much worry and not enough sleep." He paused. "Please."

It was that last word that reached down and squeezed her heart.

"Sure."

"Thanks."

The too-polite words put up a barrier. Repressed feelings lay in the lock of his jaw, the tightening of the cords in his throat.

There was no more sharing. They had both retreated, as though backing away from the edge of a precipice that would mean certain death if one took a step over it.

Caleb turned away from her, no doubt regretting how much of himself he had given away. It hurt, but she knew he acted out of self-preservation.

He sucked in air as if bracing himself against an unpalatable truth. "I've been off my game ever since...ever since it happened."

She nodded. She had an idea of what that cost him to admit.

They both needed a distraction. The case.

"I know about Jeremy Saba," she said briskly. "Is there anyone else who had it in for your brother?"

"Michael dealt with the worst of the worst. Cartel members. Money launderers. Counterfeiters. He never backed down from a case. Like I told you, there's another player on the scene, some wiseguy from Miami named Ruis Melendez."

She nodded. "Could he have been behind the murders?"

"I don't know much about him. From what Michael said, Melendez was new to the game, at least here in Atlanta. What motive would he have to take out Michael?" Caleb shook his head. "It had to be Saba. Nothing else makes sense."

A thoughtful look passed over his face.

"What is it?"

"The last time we talked, Michael said something about the linchpin. If he could take out that person, everything else would come tumbling down."

Her interest piqued, Shelley leaned forward. "Jeremy Saba?"

"I thought so."

"*Thought?* As in past tense?"

"I didn't think much about it at the time, but Michael said that Saba didn't have the brains to run that kind of operation. I thought he was trying to keep me from worrying so much by saying that Saba wasn't a real threat." Exhaling roughly, he shoved a hand through his hair. "I let myself be convinced. I was too busy playing soldier and saving the world." Self-loathing coated every syllable.

Now that she knew Caleb, she knew what the pull between duty to his country and love for his brother must have cost him. The blame he heaped upon himself was so unfair and so like him. But a man like Caleb, honorable to a fault, would always feel responsible to those he loved.

She started to tell him that when a cry tore through the shelter.

With Caleb at her side, she ran to the play area where the anguished sound had originated. Tommy cowered in the corner, eyes wide, his entire body shaking.

Standing a few feet away was a boy of similar age holding a gun.

EIGHT

Caleb swept Tommy into his arms and carried him into the kitchen. "It's all right," he said over and over. "It was pretend. A toy. It can't hurt you."

Tommy continued to scream until there was nothing left inside and the screams became hoarse sobs. Abruptly, he went silent, and his eyes looked more vacant than ever.

Finally, Caleb set Tommy down on a chair and knelt in front of him, willing Tommy to look at him, to say something, *anything*. The little boy immediately climbed off the chair and went to huddle in the corner of the room where he rocked back and forth.

Caleb's heart broke a little more with each sway of Tommy's small body. He would rather take a beating than watch his nephew wrestle with whatever nightmares were haunting him. The muscles at the nape of his neck tightened in such knots he was certain they would cut off his breathing.

Shelley came in. "How is he?" she asked quietly.

Feeling as miserable as Tommy looked, Caleb shook his head. Michael's son needed him, and he was useless. If only... The thought was lost to the bone-deep weariness that had dogged him since he'd learned of Michael's murder.

"I did my best to smooth things over out there." She placed a hand on Caleb's arm. "It's pretty plain that Tommy saw something the night his parents were killed."

He sucked in a breath. Did she know how much he needed that contact? Her soft, gentle touch grounded him.

"I know. And I have no idea what to do about it."

She wrapped her arms around his waist, and the muscles at the back of his neck started to relax. They stayed there, locked together. With a drawn-out sigh, Caleb pulled away.

He crossed the room to where Tommy continued to rock. "Come on, buddy. Let's see if we can find a game to play."

He discovered that his nephew liked checkers so they played game after silent game. Some of the tension left Tommy's body, and Caleb sent up a prayer of thanks. He'd take whatever he could get.

When it was time for lunch, Tommy sat between Caleb and Shelley. He ate a little, then padded over to where their sleeping cots were.

When Tommy's breathing evened out and his white-knuckled clutch on his bear eased, Caleb slipped out and found Shelley waiting for him in the common area.

"You know what the SEALs say?" She shook her head. "The only easy day was yesterday."

"From where I'm sitting," she said, "yesterday was no picnic."

"Nope. Somebody went and invited ants."

Shelley wanted to do some research on the various players connected to Michael's RICO case. The problem was that the shelter's one computer was a joke. It could barely send and receive email. She needed to go to her office and use the system there.

"Go," Caleb said when she told him her plan. "We'll be fine here. I want to be around when Tommy wakes up. I don't want him to be alone."

"I'll be back in a couple of hours."

After driving to within a few blocks of the office, Shelley parked the car and walked the rest of the way. Though her ankle still gave her an occasional twinge, she felt well enough to walk a short distance. She didn't know if anyone was staking out S&J's offices, but she wasn't taking any chances.

She found out what she could about Jeremy Saba and Ruis Melendez on her own, then made a call to one of her contacts in the Atlanta PD.

"We have a CI who runs in the same circles as Melendez and his crew," her friend said after an exchange of greetings. "He said that Melendez closed up shop here because the drug trade and other rackets were already sewn up."

Using criminal informants was commonplace in law enforcement. She'd used them herself when she'd been working homicide in Washington, DC. She didn't like the system, but she couldn't deny its effectiveness. In return for looking the other way on some lesser charges against a CI, the police gained information on bigger fish. It was a trade-off from which both sides benefited.

"Who did the sewing? Saba?" she asked.

"That's the thinking."

She pondered that, pinching her upper lip thoughtfully. "Thanks."

Just as she gathered up her things, including her laptop, in preparation of leaving, Sal Santonni showed up.

"Boss, there's a package for you." He handed her a box wrapped in brown paper.

"Don't worry. We scanned it. It's safe."

After slipping on a pair of latex gloves, she withdrew her pocket knife, slit the string and paper, and unwrapped the box. Inside lay several neatly stacked bundles of bills. A quick estimate made it out to be approximately $50,000.

The operative gave a low whistle. "That's some serious cash."

An envelope lay at the bottom of the box. Heart pounding, she opened it and found a note. The generic paper and computer-generated printing guaranteed that it would be nearly impossible to trace. *Walk away from Judd and the boy and more will arrive. Stay and your brother and his wife will pay.* A picture of Jake and Dani accompanied the note, a bull's-eye drawn around their faces.

Fear flooded her senses before she got hold of herself and pushed it aside. Jake would tell her to hunker down and do the job. Though she hated to interrupt his and Dani's honeymoon with such a matter, she had to call him, let him know what was going on.

Fifteen minutes later, she hung up the phone. She'd been right. Her brother had told her not to worry about him and Dani, that he would see to their safety.

"Do what you have to, sis," he said. "And kick some bad-guy butt while you're at it."

After logging in the money, note and picture, Shelley photographed them and then returned the things to the box. "Take these to the PD."

"What're you going to do?" Sal asked grimly, his eyes filled with worry.

"What I have to."

Caleb took one look at Shelley's face when she returned to the shelter and knew something had happened.

Tommy was still napping, so Caleb pointed to the common room where he and Shelley found an empty corner and sat on a threadbare sofa.

"Spill," he said.

She filled him in on the money, the note, the picture.

He weighed what he should say. "I assume you contacted Jake."

"What do you think?" The snap in her voice had him holding up his hands. "Sorry," she said. "Yes, I contacted him. Told him what's going on. He's taking Dani to a farm run by one of his buddies. They'll be safe there."

"Good. What about you?"

"What do you mean?"

"Nobody would blame you if you walked," he said, choosing his words carefully.

"I'm going to pretend you didn't say that."

Caleb pantomimed pulling his foot out of his mouth. "Now it's my turn to apologize. I know you're not afraid. Not for yourself. But this is your brother and his wife we're talking about." He swallowed the lump of emotion that had taken up residence in his throat. "I know something about that."

Her expression softened. "Jake can take care of himself and Dani. I'm not worried about them. Trying to bribe me tells me that the enemy is getting nervous. They want to isolate you and Tommy. Everything that's happened points to

Tommy knowing something they don't want found out."

"He's seven. What can he know?" Caleb had asked himself that same question over and over.

"He probably has no idea what it is. Could your brother have given Tommy something?"

"You saw what he has with him. A backpack. Some clothes. A few toys. And his bear."

"There didn't seem to be anything there," she agreed.

Something else was bothering Caleb. "How did whoever sent that package to you know you were helping me?" He didn't suspect Shelley, but it was very disconcerting that the people after Tommy always seemed to be one step ahead.

"That first night, at the motel, they had to have seen my license plate and traced it," she went on. "From there it would be easy to make the leap to S&J."

He scrubbed a hand over his face. If he'd been thinking clearly, he would have come up with the answer himself. Just another reminder that his brain wasn't firing on all cylinders.

He couldn't afford to make mistakes. Tommy's life depended on it.

NINE

"Taryn Starks, on special assignment, coming to you from outside the Atlanta courthouse. The investigation into the murders of federal prosecutor Michael Judd and his wife, Grace, is ongoing. No official statement has yet been made by the Atlanta Police Department either confirming or denying the involvement of Jeremy Saba in the murders. Saba, an alleged member of organized crime, is currently under indictment by the federal prosecutor's office.

"Here to tell us more about this heinous crime is state federal prosecutor Alfred Kruise…"

Shelley turned up the volume of the small black-and-white television that sat on the counter. Alfred Kruise, flanked by the mayor, police chief and other dignitaries, had the perfect look for public office: solid as an oak, serious as a heart attack and suave as a media star. He was king of the all-important press statement.

His face appropriately grave, he gave a slight

nod in Starks's direction. "A federal task force has been formed and is working around the clock to apprehend those responsible for the murder of Michael Judd and his wife."

Kruise's voice assumed a somber note. "Make no doubt about it—justice will be served." He cleared his throat. "This is a great loss, not only to the city but to my wife and myself, personally. Michael and Grace are...were...friends. They will be missed." He fisted a hand, and his voice once more held the ring of reassurance, that all was well and that the citizens of Atlanta need not fear. "We will not rest until the perpetrators are caught and prosecuted within the fullest extent of the law."

Shelley looked up from her task and saw that Caleb had joined her.

He hoisted a broad shoulder against a cabinet. She couldn't help noticing how attractive and virile he looked, standing there in the kitchen, filling up the space with his large, imposing form.

She turned down the volume and gestured to the television screen. "Do you think he'll make good on his promise?" she asked, more to keep Caleb talking than from any real interest in Kruise. He was a politician, and, in her experience, politicians were big on making promises but fell short in carrying them out.

"He'll try. Jeremy Saba is as slippery as they come and has a bunch of overpriced lawyers to trot out whenever he needs them. Bringing in a guilty verdict won't be easy."

She shot him a curious look. "What do you know about Kruise?"

"Not much. Michael considered him a mentor, a friend. As you know, he and Grace named Alfred and Irene Kruise Tommy's godparents."

Shelley pretended not to notice that Caleb's voice had cracked ever so slightly upon saying Michael's name. "That's a pretty big deal."

"Yeah. Michael looked up to the man, said Kruise played hardball with the lowlifes they prosecuted. Michael respected that."

The camera returned to Starks, this time in a studio setting.

She started to turn off the television when she saw a picture of Irene Kruise appear on the screen. "Now for a related story, also involving a member of the Kruise family. Irene Kruise, well-known socialite who serves on the boards of some of the Atlanta's most well-known charities, has announced that she will be hosting an auction to raise money for children who have lost their parents through violent crime."

The camera flashed to Mrs. Kruise, who was dressed with quiet understatement. "When tragedy hits close to home, as it has with our godchild, I knew I had to do something. Our auction will help children who have lost everything.

Please give until it hurts for those children who are hurting so much."

"Thank you, Mrs. Kruise," Starks said. "Now for other stories in Atlanta's social scene…"

Shelley flipped off the television.

"You don't like society news?" Caleb asked dryly.

"I don't like the reporter," Shelley said, her face creasing in a scowl. "Starks is an opportunist. When Dani was being stalked, Starks hounded her and then put out all the juicy details for everyone to gawk at. A century ago, she'd have been called a muckraker. She makes her living digging into other people's pain."

"Tell me how you really feel about the woman."

Shelley smiled as she'd known he'd meant her to, but there was no humor to be found in his face.

Caleb braced his elbows on his knees, propped his chin in his hands.

On impulse, she reached for his hand. His strong, tanned fingers linked with her smaller ones. The sight of their hands clasped in such a way moved her. She closed her eyes, allowing herself to savor the moment.

Mixing business with pleasure was never smart. They had yet to find the killers. Caleb would never give up the hunt. Neither would she. Whatever their feelings for each other, they had to be put on the back burner.

At least for now.

With those conflicting thoughts churning through her mind, she withdrew her hand.

He skimmed his fingertips against her jaw, and, without any other warning, kissed her gently. So fleeting was the kiss that she almost wondered if she'd imagined it.

But, no. It happened. It was real. Very, very real.

She drew in a deep breath, steadied herself. Caleb's kiss had scrambled her thinking, and she was struggling to make sense of the feelings spinning through her.

He pulled back. "I know. It's not the time. Or the place. And I've got no business kissing my buddy's sister."

"I didn't say that."

"No. I did."

Her gaze met his, and she saw the integrity that was so much a part of him glimmering in his eyes.

The temptation to ask him what he'd meant by the kiss, the second one they'd shared, was intense, but she resisted. As he'd said, now was not the time or the place. Soon, she prayed. Soon they would find the truth, and she and Caleb could see where this thing between them was going. Maybe, just maybe, there *was* a chance for them after all. Until then, she'd have to be patient.

Since moving to Atlanta, she'd dated a few

men, but none had touched her heart. Maybe she was old-fashioned, but she wouldn't lower her standards because a man failed to live up to them.

Until she found one who could, she was better off alone, but sometimes loneliness was a cold companion, especially when she longed for a home and family of her own.

Her thoughts took her full circle, back to Caleb. There was no doubt about it: she was in danger of losing the professional demeanor she'd worked so hard to rebuild. She couldn't give that up. Wouldn't. No matter how appealing she found her current client.

"The past has a way of coming back to haunt us, doesn't it?" Shelley asked in a musing tone. "I want to believe that I could put what happened behind me, but it won't stay put."

His gaze roamed her face. "You're trying to figure out how to rewrite history. Right?"

The man was too perceptive by half. He saw inside her, to that soft center she tried so hard to hide from everyone.

"What makes you so smart?" The question was part resentment, part admiration. "Because I understand you now. You present a tough exterior, but inside, you care. You care a lot."

He almost smiled. She saw it flicker in his intense blue eyes. Then it winked away as rapidly as it had appeared. Well, maybe it wasn't quite a smile, she amended, but at least a lessening of the lines of worry that had etched themselves at the corners of his eyes.

She wanted to keep the almost-smile there, on his face. It transformed him in unexpected ways. The next moment, she berated herself. She had no business thinking about Caleb's face, smiling or not.

"You're staring," he said.

"Sorry. Just thinking."

"Must be some pretty heavy-duty thinking."

His tone invited her to share.

"It is." She thought of the path that had brought her here. "You knew I was a cop."

At his nod, she continued. "I thought I'd seen everything there was. And then some." Memories assailed her, painting harsh pictures of waste and decay.

"I wanted to make a difference. I was assigned to the Sixth District. It was…rough."

Rough was an understatement for the blocks in the district, where boarded-up houses, graffiti-covered buildings and cannibalized cars were the norm rather than the exception. At night, street corners were populated with dealers and buyers, furtive eyes on the make for cops and predators. Pops of gunfire were as commonplace as the buzz of mosquitoes.

There was nothing neat or nice about police work. It was messy, dirty and too often heart-breaking. She'd stuck it out, not for the commendations and promotions but because she believed in the work even when it left raw sores upon her soul.

"I did it for as long as I could until I realized I was in danger of losing my sanity along with my humanity. Then, I heard about training for the Service. So I decided, 'Why not?'"

"It couldn't have been easy."

Her derisive laugh was aimed at herself for her naïveté. "No. I worked my rear off to qualify. Then came the hard stuff."

"You loved it."

She nodded. "One of my supervisors took an interest in me, gave me a leg up. I was on my way. Or so I thought. And then everything came crashing down.

"I was seeing another agent at the time. Jeffrey." A sad smile flitted across her mouth. "We knew we had to break it off. Relationships between agents were strictly forbidden, but we kept telling ourselves that we could do the job and not let our feelings for each other get in the way."

Caleb's eyes never left her. "But they did."

Her time with Jeffrey had been complicated. They'd enjoyed each other's company and had a mutual respect for each other's work. For all its strengths, though, it had been a fragile relationship, and it had broken into thousands of pieces when she was promoted over him.

She took a deep breath and squared her shoulders in preparation for saying what came next.

"I was moving up the ranks at a fast pace. Jeffrey was jealous. He wanted to make me look bad." She drew in another breath. She could do this. All she had to do was say the words very fast, get them out in the open. "Because of our relationship, I took his word on a threat assessment when I should have checked the facts out for myself. A good man died because of that."

"The jerk used you."

It warmed her that Caleb had immediately taken her side. He barely knew her, didn't know Jeffrey at all, and still Caleb had championed her.

She supposed that Jeffrey had tried to be glad for her when she'd first been promoted. However, support had quickly turned to snarky comments and escalated into an ugly jealousy. By the time of their last post, he had stopped taking orders from her at all and then had sabotaged the mission. The result was that he had given her faulty information, information which had cost the life of a good agent as well as his own.

Why hadn't she seen through the handsome exterior to the shallow and vengeful man at his core? Had she been so desperate to love and to be loved that she'd blinded herself to the evil that lurked inside? The man whom she'd thought might be *the one* had betrayed her in the worst way possible.

"I was absolved of blame officially, but unofficially, I knew I was finished. I couldn't stay after what happened. Even if others didn't blame me, I blamed myself." She paused. "I still do."

"Like Jake blamed himself for what happened overseas?"

"That's different," she said automatically. Her brother had thrown the same challenge at her, pointing out that if she wanted him to forgive himself for the deaths of his buddies, that she needed to do the same.

"Is it?"

She thought about it. "I knew I was breaking the rules. I let it affect my judgment."

"You're human."

"The rules are there for a reason," she argued.

"You did the best you could. Don't beat yourself up over it."

"It was my fault. I took someone else's word for something I should have checked out myself. My partner died because I was gullible." She made a sound that was part anger, part pain.

"You think you let your partner down. That's nonsense, and you know it. You're taking refuge in guilt when you should be grateful that you're alive."

"You're right. By all rights, I should be dead along with my friend." She exhaled a shaky breath. "But I lived. Maybe that's what's eating me up inside."

"We're not so different."

"No?" Her brow wrinkled in question.

"We're both wearing our guilt like a coat of armor."

"Not a pretty picture," she said with a wry twist to her lips. "Not in Georgia."

For a long time after she'd left the Service, she'd doubted herself. Her confidence had been shaken, and she didn't know if she still had the edge she'd once honed so carefully. She was cautious to a fault, even fearful, until Jake had reminded her that she was cheating not only her clients but herself when she didn't give her best.

With that, the fog had cleared from her mind. She no longer questioned her abilities, but she couldn't get past blaming herself. With the Lord's help, she was stronger now, more sure of herself, her place in life.

"Let it go," Caleb said softly.

Recognizing her words to him, she tried to smile but failed miserably. "I wish I could, but I can't. I should have realized how twisted Jeffrey had become, but all I could think about was climbing the next rung on the ladder.

"If I could go back, I'd have done things differently. I would have made sure that Jeffrey got help. I certainly wouldn't have believed him. I would have checked things out for myself. Because of me, a good man, a husband and father, died." Tears roughened her voice.

"You didn't kill your friend. You trusted a fellow agent. You're too hard on yourself." He skimmed a finger down her cheek, the gesture as gentle as the touch of a butterfly wing.

Was she? She didn't know. All she knew was that she had let the Service and herself down. She didn't make excuses for her actions. Her fallen friend deserved better.

For some reason, she felt compelled to share the rest of it with Caleb. Still, she hesitated. Why was it so hard to say out loud? Why was the pain so fresh that it could have happened yesterday rather than several years ago? There wasn't a day that went by that she didn't remember...

"I'm the one who shot Jeffrey." Her dispassionate tone mocked the myriad of emotions roiling through her, and she offered a tight smile.

Taking a life wasn't something to be taken lightly. Unfortunately, television and movies too frequently portrayed law enforcement personnel as trigger-happy and irresponsible. The truth was, it sometimes came down to the reluctant but necessary use of force.

Though she'd been furious at Jeffrey's betrayal, she'd never wanted him dead, even when his actions had caused another agent's death. "He turned his gun on me. I didn't have a choice."

She risked a glance at Caleb. She thought he might try to stop her recitation, but he only gazed at her with understanding and respect.

"Maybe you should practice what you preach," he said gently. "Start forgiving yourself for being human."

Her nod was part rueful acknowledgment, part chagrin that he had used her own words against her. "You're right. I'm hardly in a position to preach forgiveness."

For all her fine words, she had no right to tell Caleb to forgive himself. Not when guilt weighed on her heart like a millstone.

"A shooting review board was held. I was cleared of any wrongdoing, but it didn't matter. I became a pariah in Washington. My colleagues and my friends suddenly were too busy for me. They closed ranks. Once an agent has a black mark on her record, she's done."

Pain washed over her as she recalled the guarded looks her onetime friends gave her, the uneasy smiles that told her others were uncomfortable in her presence. Memories were long in the nation's capital.

After the review board, her supervisor had told her to take some time off, to get her head together; in fact, he insisted upon it. For her own good, of course. Did she need to see a counselor? A psychiatrist? She'd get the very best. Everyone was on her side, she was assured over and over. When things calmed down, she could return. Not to worry, the Service stood behind its own.

It was all window-dressing.

She was out. She could read the writing on the wall as well as anyone. "It was only a matter of time before I was reassigned, stuck in a cubicle, buried in some outpost and wondering where my career had gone. I knew I had to get out of town while I still had a shred of dignity."

"Why Atlanta?"

Her smile was wry. "You'll think it's foolish."

"Try me."

"I saw *Gone with the Wind* when I was twelve years old and fell in love with the movie. When I was a bit older, I realized what I'd really fallen in love with was the idea of a city rebuilding itself after nearly being destroyed."

"And you wanted to rebuild yourself after your career ended and decided Atlanta was the place to do it."

He got it. How many people would understand why she'd done what she had? His respect and warmth empowered Shelley, as though sharing that part of her life had purged the anger and guilt and self-pity.

She hadn't told anyone—not even Jake—the entire story, keeping the details locked deep inside her, not realizing how they still haunted her. Her heart suddenly felt lighter because Caleb had drawn the story from her in a way no one else had been able to do.

"You're pretty smart," she said.

"You're pretty smart yourself."

"We're in agreement. We're two pretty smart people."

She was gratified to see him smile, and she felt a kinship with him that was beyond comprehension.

"Law enforcement was all I knew," Shelley said in answer to the question reflected in his eyes. "There's a need for high-level protection these days, with all the kidnappings and ransom demands in the business world. I was a natural, and when Jake got home, I asked him to join me." She shrugged. "We aren't getting rich with it, but we do all right."

"No wonder Jake is proud of you," Caleb murmured, his gaze filled with warmth.

A rush of pleasure skittered through her, but she couldn't go there. Not now. Mixing the job with her personal life was a recipe for disaster. Hadn't she learned anything from the past?

She'd gotten involved with Jeffrey, had let it cloud her judgment, and two men were dead because of it. Granted, the circumstances with Caleb were different, but it didn't change the facts.

Feelings didn't belong on the job. Period.

So why didn't that make her feel any better?

With effort, she tore her eyes from his. Glanced out the kitchen window. The rain was on hold, but there was an anticipation in the air, as if something were pent up and just waiting to happen.

Caleb spent the night thinking about what he needed to do.

"I want to go to the Marshals' office," he told Shelley the following morning as they scrambled several dozen eggs for breakfast. "I need to find out more about the two marshals assigned to guard Michael's family." He paused. "Will you stay with Tommy?"

"My job is to protect both of you."

"Come on, Shelley," he growled. "You and I both know that I'm more than capable of fending for myself." She started to say something, but he held up a hand. "Right now, I need you to take care of Tommy. End of story."

After breakfast and seeing that Tommy was settled in a playgroup with other children, Caleb drove to the federal building, relieved to be doing something. *Anything.* Inaction didn't sit well with him.

As a member of Delta, he'd excelled at walking through a problem and coming out at the other end with a solution, but the only thing he could think about now was protecting Tommy and finding out who had murdered Michael and Grace. He didn't have an answer to either.

Caleb had met the supervisory marshal in the

Atlanta US Marshals' office on one of his rare visits to Michael and family. Grant Amachker was on the wrong side of forty, but carried his years well. Sparse gray hair framed a face that spoke of a lifetime of outdoor work.

The two men shook hands. Caleb felt the power the other man gave to the grip. Amachker was obviously a formidable man and wanted Caleb to know it.

"Thank you for seeing me," Caleb said. His gaze moved around the room, taking in the framed certificates and photographs on the wall. One item caught his interest: a picture of Amachker with some army buddies. By the look of it, it was over twenty years old.

"I wish it were under different circumstances."

There was no good answer to that, so Caleb didn't attempt one.

Amachker scrubbed a hand across his jaw. "Your brother was one of the good guys. His rep was spotless."

Caleb dipped his head, but that wasn't why he was here. He already knew Michael's reputation was unblemished. "Thanks. What do you know about the two marshals assigned to guard Michael's family?"

"They're both on the job for years. I chose the best for the assignment." The marshal's voice sounded as ragged as Caleb felt.

"Still. Somehow the killers managed to get through the marshal on guard that night. What do you know about Victoria Ramiherison?" His gaze bore into Amachker.

"Got ten years' experience here, before that, she worked at the ATF. Glowing reports from all her superiors." Amachker narrowed his eyes. "She's got a goose egg at the base of her skull, where she was hit trying to protect your brother and sister-in-law."

"Why didn't they kill her, like they did Michael and Grace?" Caleb got the words out even though they wanted to stick in his throat and choke him. Would he ever get used to the fact that his brother was dead?

Amachker scowled. "If you're trying to say Ramiherison's dirty, you're barking up the wrong tree. Her record's so clean you could eat off it. No reason to think she'd turn." He rocked back on his heels once. Twice.

"Money's a powerful motivator," Caleb thought aloud.

"We're checking her and Matheson out," Amachker said, naming the other marshal assigned to guard Michael's family. "We'll find out what we already know: they aren't dirty. They'll be tarnished all the same." His features darkened, and his brows slammed together. "You need to let us do our job."

Like you already did? Caleb didn't voice his thoughts, but they must have been plain on his face, for Amachker nodded, all pretense of friendliness now gone. His face morphed into a hard mask.

"Yeah, I know. But that doesn't mean you can go all Rambo and take things into your own hands. There are procedures to follow." The sudden dislike in his voice ricocheted around the room like a stray bullet.

"Never lost anyone on my watch before," Amachker said in a tight voice. "It changes things."

"Yeah," Caleb retorted and let his stare burn into the man for another minute. "I'd like to meet Matheson and Ramiherison."

"Matheson's here. Ramiherison's still out on sick leave." Amachker tapped a couple of buttons on his phone. "Send in Matheson."

Less than a minute later, Marshal Matheson came in the room. "You wanted me, sir?"

"Matheson, I'd like you to meet Caleb Judd. Michael Judd's brother."

Matheson extended his hand. "I'm sorry for your loss, Judd. Your brother was a good man. A credit to the law enforcement community."

"Thank you." If there was any deceit in the man's face, Caleb failed to detect it. "Can you tell me anything about that night?"

Matheson shook his head. "I was sick that

night. Some kind of stomach virus. I was fine, and then I wasn't."

"You didn't try to get someone to fill in for you?"

"I tried," the marshal said, the heat in his voice betraying temper. "But we're shorthanded as it is. Budget cuts. You can't know how much I wish I had been there."

"I think I can," Caleb murmured.

"Sorry. I wasn't thinking."

"If you can think of anything, anything at all, I'd appreciate you letting me know."

"I'll do that." Matheson stumbled, brushing up against Caleb as he left the office. "Sorry."

Caleb made to leave, then stopped. "One more thing," he said to Amachker. "At one time, Michael said something about a Ruis Melendez. What can you tell me about him?"

"He's a midlevel player from Miami. He's got juice and was trying to get himself a crew put together here in Atlanta. Things must have fizzled out for him, though, because we haven't heard anything about him lately." Amachker's eyes narrowed. "Did Michael tell you anything else?"

"No."

Caleb took his leave after that.

Outside, the sun glinted off something in the truck's undercarriage. The vehicle was more rust than shine, and Caleb bent to take a look. What he saw had him backing up slowly.

His specialty wasn't in bomb disposal, but he had enough experience in the field to recognize the device attached to the truck. He also knew he couldn't defuse the bomb himself.

Caleb retraced his steps to the Marshals' headquarters. "We've got a problem."

TEN

The shelter was alive with activity in the afternoon. At Reverend Monson's insistence, Cassie Travers, a therapist who volunteered at the shelter two days a week, used his office for her therapy sessions.

Tommy had seen something the night of his parents' murder. Shelley was certain of it. It was the most likely explanation for his silence, a shock so profound that it had forced him into a safe place where nothing could reach him.

"Shelley, could you take over the children's story time?" Pastor Monson asked. "Our regular person is down with the flu. It'd be a real help if you could fill in."

She would have rather walked barefoot over burning coals, but she found herself agreeing. She owed the pastor.

Pastor Monson introduced her to the children and reminded them of their manners.

Shelley picked up a thick book of fairy tales, and started reading.

"And they lived happily ever after," she concluded an hour later.

"There's no such thing as a happy ending," a red-haired girl who looked around eight said in a loud voice. There was a certain insistency in the girl's voice that gave Shelley pause.

Fortunately, Pastor Monson arrived at that moment. "Children, please thank Ms. Rabb for reading to you today."

"Thank you," twelve children parroted, all except the red-haired girl.

"You have the rest of them fooled with your stories, but not me. Happy endings are for suckers."

"Cherry, it's time for chores."

"Okay, Pastor." The little girl took herself off but not before giving Shelley a final challenging look.

Shelley searched for something to say. "She seems very mature for her age."

"That's Cherry Parker. She and her brother have been here about a month. They arrived with the clothes on their back and nothing else. Ordinarily, they'd be handed over to Child Protection Services, but I asked for and was granted permission to keep them here. I knew Cassie could help them more than CPS could. They're overworked and understaffed."

Sensing that there was more to the story, Shelley asked, "What happened?"

Pastor Monson's expression grew grave. "Her parents left Cherry and her brother in a motel room. Somehow, Cherry got them here."

"How old is her brother?"

"Five."

Shelley turned away, gathering up the books.

"It hurts you, doesn't it?" the pastor asked quietly. "Hearing about Cherry and her brother."

"No." Shelley kept her face averted, busying herself with stacking the books on a shelf. "Why should it?" she asked in a voice she couldn't quite make sound normal.

"Because you understand."

She was about to deny the charge, but Cassie appeared at that moment. "I sent Tommy to help with chores."

"I'll leave you ladies to talk," Pastor Monson said and withdrew.

Shelley put the pastor's question and the memories it evoked out of her mind. "What did you find out?"

"My guess is that Tommy saw something so horrible that when he buried it, he also buried his ability to talk."

Though Shelley was gratified to have her guess confirmed by an expert, they were no closer to learning what he saw or how to help him. "What can we do for him?"

"Short answer…be patient." Cassie smiled at Shelley's grimace. "Whatever's keeping him from talking is so huge that it's bottled up his words inside him. When that block dissolves, the words will spill out of him so fast that they'll trip over each other."

Despite the seriousness of the subject, Shelley couldn't help an inward smile at Cassie's front porch Southern drawl. Ever since Shelley had made Atlanta her home, she'd delighted in the nuances of the language and the melodic sounds that the most ordinary of words could produce.

She shook her head at her own musings and focused on what Cassie had said.

"How long?"

Cassie didn't mince words. "Maybe tomorrow. Maybe two weeks from now. Maybe two years. I'll work with him every chance I get, but there're no guarantees."

"Thanks for seeing him."

"I wish there were more I could do."

Shelley bit back her disappointment. Somehow, despite her best efforts to keep her distance, she'd developed feelings for the little boy. Finding the key to unlock his words had become important in an intensely personal way.

What had started as a routine job had turned into something far more complex. Her determination to keep her relationship with Caleb and

Tommy on a professional basis had eroded with every day she spent with them.

Despite his pain at the death of his brother and sister-in-law, Caleb had taken on caring for Tommy with his whole heart. That kind of devotion was rare these days. She wanted to learn more about Caleb Judd the man, outside of the investigation.

Until…unless…they learned the truth about what happened the night Michael and Grace were murdered, she feared there would be no chance for her and Caleb to discover more about each other.

No chance at all.

Caleb was transported back to Afghanistan where IEDs or other kinds of bombs littered the landscape. He'd watched as buddies had been injured or killed. Sometimes he wondered which was worse. He shook his head, trying to wipe the images from his mind.

In the end, the bomb was defused without incident, the vehicle impounded, the crisis over. At least for now.

If there was anything a soldier feared, it was an adversary who was willing to do whatever it took to come out on top. Planting a bomb in the truck took things to a whole new level. If it had exploded, the bomb would have killed not just Caleb but anyone in a sixty-foot radius.

A four-hour interrogation by Amachker and a detective from the Atlanta PD ended with Caleb holding on to his temper by a thread, especially after he butted heads with Amachker.

"You had a close call," the marshal said with an I-told-you-so air. "Maybe now you'll stop playing detective and let us do our job."

"Yeah? Maybe if your people had been doing *their* jobs, Michael and Grace would still be alive." Caleb realized he'd stepped over the line, but he couldn't bring himself to apologize.

"You've been through a rough time, so I'm going to let that pass," Amachker said evenly, leveling a cold gaze on Caleb. "This is a federal case. Leave it to the professionals."

Once more, Caleb kept his temper in check. It wouldn't do any good to antagonize the Marshals' office any more than he already had.

With an assurance that he wouldn't be leaving town, he departed. He had to get back to the shelter. Without a vehicle, he found a metro station and hopped on a train. He had an awful lot to tell Shelley.

Five hours after he'd left the shelter, he returned to find her snuggled with Tommy on a battered sofa reading to him. The homey sight momentarily wiped away the stress and anxiety of the past few hours.

Shelley took one look at Caleb but wisely kept her questions until later. "Tommy, why don't you and I go see what Pastor Monson is doing? He might need some help."

Within a few minutes, she returned. "What happened?"

"You may want to get in your car and not look back when you hear what happened."

ELEVEN

"A bomb?" Shelley kept her voice low. Kitchen sounds drowned out their voices; still, she didn't want to chance anyone else hearing. "You're fortunate you saw it. Even more so that you're alive."

The rueful twist of her lips mirrored his own feelings. "Like I said, you may want to rethink the job. You didn't sign on for any of this, first the threat to Jake and Dani...and now a bomb."

"That's the second time you've accused me of wanting to cut and run. When are you going to get it through your thick skull that I'm sticking?" Not giving him a chance to answer, she huffed, "Now that we've gotten *that* out of the way, let's decide what we're going to do."

"With you on my side, how can I lose?"

"You have the Lord on your side. That's enough."

Caleb drew her to him, tipping her head back and looking into her eyes. "All the same, I'm glad you're here."

"So am I."

The next thought that hit her made her features turn hard. "That was a stupid play on their part."

"How so?"

"If the bomb killed you, all well and good." At Caleb's droll expression, she waved her hand. "You know what I mean. Bombs are unpredictable. Something could have set it off before you got in the car. But you weren't killed, and now you're more determined than ever to get at the truth.

"That's what I meant by it being stupid. They should know that a man like you wouldn't be scared off."

"Thanks," he said with a wry twist of his lips. "I think."

Their enemies had upped the game with the planting of the bomb. She, Caleb and Tommy couldn't continue hiding at the shelter. She wouldn't risk the people here. She said as much, and Caleb agreed.

"Where do we head to now?"

"My place. Neither Jake's nor my names are listed on any paperwork." The house was held by a holding company, something she and Jake set up deliberately.

She explained what was happening to Pastor Monson. "I can't take the risk that whoever is after us will find us here."

The pastor nodded. "My prayers are with you."

"Thank you, Pastor. Thank you for everything. I'll be in touch with plans for the benefit."

Within an hour, the three of them had moved to Shelley's house. The homey-looking bungalow had a top-notch security system that Shelley and Jake had designed themselves.

Maybe she should have brought them here in the first place. She strove to keep her professional life and private life separate, but this wasn't the first time she or Jake had brought a client into her home. Jake had brought Dani here when she was being stalked.

Shelley asked herself why she'd resisted doing the same with Tommy and Caleb. The answer she came up with didn't make her feel any better: she was afraid of where such a move would lead. Her relationship with Caleb had already crossed the line between business and personal. Taking him to her home blurred the boundaries even more.

After a quick dinner of burgers and fries she and Caleb had picked up on the way, they settled Tommy in the guestroom.

"Planting the bomb took some planning," Shelley said, thinking aloud. "How did whoever did it know you'd show up at the federal building at that time?"

"Good question. I've been asking myself the same thing. The only thing I could come up with was that they figured I'd head there at some point looking for answers."

She thought of what that meant. "That means someone has the Marshals' office staked out."

"That's the only thing that makes sense." Absently, Caleb thrust his hand in his pocket and came away with a folded piece of paper. He smoothed it out, then read aloud. "Peachtree and 7th. 11:00 p.m."

"Where did that come from?"

"Back at the fed building, one of the marshals stumbled against me. I didn't think anything of it at the time, but now I get it. He wanted to pass this to me without anyone knowing about it."

She didn't waste any time. "I'll get one of my operatives to stay with Tommy, and we'll go hear what the marshal has to say."

"You're going with me?"

"You got that right."

Once more, Caleb gave thanks that Shelley was on his side. She arranged for one of her people to watch Tommy, and within an hour, they were on their way to the meeting place.

They arrived early and did a reconnaissance of the area. It was a warehouse district and appeared deserted.

The darkened interior of the car provided an unexpected intimacy. The air turned thick, hard to breathe. There were things he wanted to say to her, things he didn't have the right to say.

It never seemed to be the right time or place, he thought with a grimace.

He studied her hand. Such small, elegant hands, but they did the job. Though her hands were tiny, her heart was not, and he wondered if she had any idea how huge that heart truly was.

His emotions felt strung like tightly wound barbed wire, prickly and exposed. Worry over Tommy mixed with unexpected feelings for Shelley. She intrigued him more than any woman he'd met in years.

This was a woman who brought everything to the table, including a compassionate nature and a kind heart. When he was with her, he forgot that he topped her by nearly a foot. Her spirit was so big, so dauntless, so courageous, that she filled whatever space she happened to find herself in.

She deserved a man who appreciated her strength, her faith, her spirit. *A man like me.* The thought didn't disturb him as it once might have. Instead, it felt right. In the next moment, he felt like a piece of scum. What was he doing, thinking of a future with Shelley, when Tommy was still in danger?

The sound of the door opening cut his thoughts short.

Matheson slid into the backseat. "Who's she?" he asked, pointing to Shelley.

"A friend," Caleb said curtly. "What's with all the cloak-and-dagger stuff?"

"Your visit set something in motion today."

"If by setting things in motion you mean having a bomb put in my car, you're right."

"They're running scared." The marshal darted a look over his shoulder, as though he expected the mysterious goons to be watching him.

"Who's *they*?"

The marshal took a long time in answering. "Your brother wasn't taken out because of Saba."

"What do you mean?" Shelley asked, joining the conversation for the first time.

"There's a big-scale operation going on. A lot more than what a slickster wiseguy like Saba can pull off. Witnesses are disappearing. Just last month, a safe house was blown up. And then your brother and his wife. Should never have happened. But it did."

Caleb digested this. "You're saying the marshals' office has a mole?"

"Not just us. It's a virus that's spread throughout the ranks. The DEA. The FBI. Even the locals. Last year an undercover detective was made. He was found with his neck slit. Drug busts gone south because the right person was tipped off. Someone's selling the bunch of us down the river, and we're too dumb to stop it."

"Things happen."

"Yeah. But not like this." Exhaling roughly,

Matheson shoved a hand through his hair. "People are starting to ask questions."

"People like Michael."

The other man's silence answered for him. "Whoever's behind this is wired in tight to someone important," he said at last. "They're always one step ahead of us."

Matheson's words echoed what Caleb thought.

"Wired tight to who? Someone at the Marshals'? At the Bureau? Give me something."

"If I knew, I'd be doing something. But I don't. No one does, but they're having a real good laugh at our expense.

"I've been doing this job for twenty-three years," the marshal said after a few more moments of silence. "A couple more and I can retire. But right now, I'm thinking of hanging it up. I won't get my full pension, but at least I'll still be alive."

He sent Caleb a knowing look. "I get what you're thinking. That I'm a coward. Maybe so. But I've got a grandson. He's just two, but in another couple of years, he'll be old enough to play catch." Furrows of worry gathering between his brows, he sighed heavily. "I want to be there for him. I want to be able to throw a ball to him and watch him catch it."

"I don't think you're a coward." Caleb let his gaze meet that of the marshal in the mirror.

"A coward wouldn't have come here to warn

us. I think you're fed up because you don't know who you can trust."

"Is there anyone, anyone at all, you trust?" Shelley asked, and Caleb saw her watching the marshal just as he had.

Matheson shook his head.

"Not even your own people?"

His eyes looked bleak. "No."

Caleb understood why the marshal would consider resigning. If you couldn't trust those people who were supposed to have your back, how were you supposed to put your life on the line day after day?

Though it was for vastly different reasons, he thought of his own struggle in deciding whether or not to resign from Delta. He was now Tommy's guardian. Could he perform those duties and remain with his unit?

Caleb shelved that for the moment and focused on Matheson.

The marshal rubbed his temples. "I told you that the night your brother and his wife were killed, I was sick."

"Pretty convenient," Caleb commented, his earlier suspicions returning.

"If you're thinking I ducked out on duty because I knew something was going to happen, you're wrong. But..."

"But what?"

"I'm wondering if someone was trying to get

me out of the way. At the time, I was too busy barfing my guts out to think about anything else, but now I've got to wonder."

"What are you saying?" Caleb asked.

"At first, I thought it was some kind of virus. Then I started to think maybe something I'd eaten was off. The way it came on, real sudden like, it seemed more like food poisoning."

"You think someone deliberately poisoned you?" Shelley asked, her tone thoughtful.

"I'm saying it's possible."

Caleb thought through the implications. "Who had the opportunity?"

"I was at the safe house all day, with your brother and his family." A beat of silence went by, then another. "And Ramiherison."

"You see anybody else that day?"

The marshal shook his head. "That was it." Once more, he met Caleb's gaze in the mirror. "Man, I can't tell you how rotten I feel about your brother and his wife. If I'd known what was going to go down, I'd have been there, even though I was hanging over the toilet the whole night."

The two men shared a look of understanding, both having pledged their lives to making the world a better place.

"What can we do?" Caleb asked.

"Watch your back." Matheson opened the car

door. "If you tell anyone about this conversation, I'll deny it."

Caleb nodded. "Fair enough."

But Matheson was already gone.

TWELVE

A stray wisp of sunlight managed to slip through
the kitchen window.

Shelley watched the play of light as it danced
across the floor, its capricious path dictated by
the movement of the blinds which, in turn, was
caused by the faint breeze stirred by the window AC unit.

Once more, she mulled over the meeting last
night with Matheson. Agents with the Secret Service were schooled in the art of deciphering micro-
expressions, tiny, nearly indiscernible movements
in the face that revealed people's true feelings,
rather than those they voiced aloud. Her training
had made noticing such things an instinct, an instinct that had saved her life and that of others on
more than one occasion.

She'd studied Matheson through the rearview
mirror last night, trying to decide if he was playing straight with her and Caleb, and had come

away with the conclusion that he was telling the truth.

The marshal had been scared; that was plain. In the end, it turned out he'd had a right to be. She recalled what he'd said of wanting to play ball with his grandson. It wasn't a big dream; it was an ordinary one.

The following morning, the lead news story had been a grim one. Looking appropriately grave, Taryn Starks reported, "A United States marshal was gunned down in the warehouse district last night. More details to follow after this message."

Caleb and Shelley had exchanged looks over the breakfast table.

"I don't believe in coincidences," she said.

He put down his fork and wiped his face with a napkin. "Neither do I."

Matheson would never get to make his dream come true or see his grandson grow up. She wished she and Caleb could have done something—anything—to protect him.

Matheson's murder had ratcheted up the threat. Again. She knew Caleb wanted to go on the offensive.

The hours of inaction, of waiting and worrying, had worn on him. Although still devastatingly handsome, new lines scored his forehead, while the shadows under his eyes seemed to have multiplied overnight. The brackets at the corners of his mouth deepened, thinning his lips into an uncompromising line.

"I'm going to see Victoria Ramiherison," he announced. "She's involved. I know it. I have to find out what she knows. Before…"

Shelley understood what he hadn't said. Before Ramiherison was killed, as well.

She had known this was coming. She'd already thought it through and knew what she had to do. "Whoever put that bomb in your car and killed Matheson will be waiting for you. They know what you look like. They won't expect me."

"Don't you get it?" he bit out. "Someone tried to blow me up. They murdered Matheson. They don't care who they hurt, who they kill. Whoever gets in their way is just collateral damage. You being a woman won't make a difference." Caleb gave her a hard-eyed stare.

She pushed it right back at him. With interest. "I can take care of myself. I always have."

"You're not going. Not alone."

Shelley practically felt the vertebrae of her spine snap into place one by one. She took a breath before she said something they'd both regret. "What about when you went to the fed building yesterday? *Alone*."

"That's…" He broke off.

"Different? Is that what you were going to say?"

"Yeah. It's different."

"And how is it different? Because you're a man and I'm a woman?"

"Of course not." But his voice lacked conviction.

"Then what is it? Because from where I'm sitting, that's exactly what it looks like." She let him think about that. "This is who I am, what I do. If you can't accept that, then we're better off knowing now."

"You've got it all wrong."

She fisted her hands, planted them on her hips. "Do I? Or do you just accept the parts of me that fit in with your idea of what you think I should be?"

"I accept everything you are. You are the strongest woman I've ever known. You matter to me."

The unexpected words ambushed her, defusing much of the hurt. She had none to give in return. She didn't know how she felt about Caleb. Too much? Not enough? The inner battle waged inside her.

When Tommy came out of the guest room, rubbing his eyes, holding his bear and looking heartbreakingly vulnerable, she and Caleb shelved the argument, but she knew it was far from over.

Words, those said and those left unsaid, simmered between them. But their anger was set aside as they saw to the boy. While Caleb helped Tommy shower and dress, she prepared breakfast.

"Chocolate chip pancakes," she said, presenting them with a flourish when man and boy returned a short while later.

Tommy's blank stare didn't waver. He sat, picked up a fork and ate mechanically. When he was done, he looked at Caleb, who nodded. Tommy picked up his bear and headed back to the bedroom.

"He's hurting, and I can't do a thing to stop it," Caleb muttered, his gaze trailing after Tommy.

"That's why we have to find answers," Shelley said gently. "Tommy needs the truth. Maybe then he can face what happened." She hesitated. "I'll go to Ramiherison's, get her to talk to me, and we'll be a step closer to finding the truth."

"How're you going to do that?"

"I can be pretty persuasive when I want to be." Shelley tried a smile, but it wasn't returned. "This is my job, Caleb. It's who I am. You and Tommy won't be safe until we find the truth about what happened to his parents."

"Send one of your operatives."

"And ask someone else to take the risk because I won't?"

He seized on the last word. "So you admit there's risk involved."

She blew out an exasperated breath. "Of course there's risk! Crossing the street is a risk."

"But people usually aren't shooting at you or trying to blow you up when you're crossing the street."

She'd had enough. "Protecting you and Tommy is my job. I can't do that if you don't trust me."

"It's not a question of trust."

"Isn't it?" she challenged.

"You go in, talk to her and get out. Nothing more."

His brusque order grated, and those tingling hackles threatened once more, but she nodded. "I'll be fine." She scribbled a number on a piece of paper. "This is Sal's number. Call him if you need anything."

When Caleb didn't respond, she asked, "Do you trust me?"

"Of course."

"Then trust me to do my best. Trust my instincts and my training."

She'd stopped him with that. She saw it in his face.

"I know you're highly trained," he said, a muscle ticking in his jaw. "But if something happened to you…" Reaching for her, he rested his forehead against hers.

Waves of worry pulsed from him. While she was warmed at his concern for her, she couldn't allow it to prevent her from doing her job the best way she knew how. He lifted his head, his gaze fixed on her, his eyes dark eyes smoldering with something she couldn't identify.

If Caleb couldn't accept…and respect…her professionalism, she knew that any possibility of a future relationship with him was out of the question. She had already suffered because of a man who didn't respect her or her abilities. She wouldn't put herself through that again.

Shelley stuck with her plan, but she knew Caleb wasn't happy. The worry lines between his heavy brows hadn't relaxed; if anything, they'd increased. His face was all hard planes and sharp angles.

"Jeffrey didn't trust me," she said quietly. "He didn't trust that I could do the job as well as any man. He didn't want to believe that I was as good at the job as he was. It twisted something inside him. In the end, it destroyed him."

"I'm not Jeffrey."

"Then let me do my job."

Her voice stopped short of pleading. She wouldn't beg for his respect. That wasn't her way. Though he'd agreed with her plan, she sensed the barrier between them. Unless he saw her for the woman she was, that distance would only grow and slowly destroy whatever they might have.

"You're the bravest woman I've ever met," he said huskily. "I'd go into battle with you in a heartbeat."

From a soldier, an army Delta no less, those were high words of praise.

"You'll be careful," he said, his eyes glittering with emotion.

"Of course."

Her breath caught in her throat, and she noticed the dark length of his eyelashes, the strong line of his jaw. She didn't dare think beyond the mission.

He took her hand, linking his strong, tanned fingers with her smaller ones, and pressed a kiss to her palm.

Caleb wasn't one to wear his heart on his sleeve. Had he confused gratitude with love? And what of her? She admired him, respected him. But admiration and respect didn't equal love, either.

Then, too, he didn't know what he wanted to do with the rest of his life. And when it came right down to it, neither did she. Having her own protection/security company was great, but she wanted, needed, more.

She drew in a deep breath, steadied herself.

He pulled back. "I know. It's not the time. Or the place."

"I didn't say that."

"No. I did." He smoothed his hand to her cheek. "When this is over…"

The promise in the words sent a flutter to

her heart, and she nodded. "When this is over."
Would they ever be able to make good on it?

Soon, she prayed. When the job was over,
maybe, just maybe, there was a chance for them.
Until then, she'd have to be patient.

Once more, he bent his head to brush his lips
over hers. The world went away. All that mattered was the touch of his mouth on hers.

The sweetness of the moment seemed to go
on forever. With a start, she realized she didn't
want it to end. In Caleb's arms, she felt as if she'd
come home.

When he lifted his head, his gaze warm on
her, a rush of feeling poured through her, and
she knew she had been waiting all her life for
this moment, this man.

And, regretfully, she pulled back.

They had yet to identify the man who had
given the kill order. Caleb would never give up
the hunt, and neither would she. Whatever their
feelings for each other, they had to be put on the
back burner. For now.

Maybe forever.

He kissed her lightly. The brush of his lips was
as ephemeral as the touch of a butterfly wing,
but so very real.

She hadn't planned this thing between them.
She certainly hadn't wanted it. But it had happened. What was the saying? The heart wants

what the heart wants, and her heart wanted this man.

"I'll be back when I can."

"You're still going?"

She stared at him in amazement. "Of course I am. Is that why you kissed me? To control me?" A pain-barbed thorn cut through her heart.

Anger and censure tightened the corners of his mouth. "No. But I thought…"

"Thought that if you showed me that you cared that I'd change my mind? It doesn't work that way, Caleb. It's time to put an end to this. You and Tommy need answers."

"And you? What do you need?"

Unable to answer, she walked away.

After making sure that Tommy was occupied with an electronic game he'd found in Shelley's bookcase, Caleb sat at the kitchen table, removed his gun and set about cleaning it. The task was soothing in its familiarity because he'd performed it countless times before. When you were fighting the enemy, you didn't have time to stop and think about how to reload your gun. You simply did it.

Shelley's reaction to his objections of her going on her own stung, there was no getting around it. All of the muscles in his shoulders and neck bunched. His fingers tightened around the grip of the pistol. Deliberately, he relaxed the muscles, unclenched his fingers.

His task done, Caleb put away the weapon and tapped his fingers against the table.

Once more, he wished he hadn't behaved as he had when Shelley had told him of her plan. He should have understood that his questioning her ability triggered bad memories. But when she'd compared him to the man who'd betrayed her, Caleb had seen red. Truth be known, insult still bloomed hot and bright in memory as resentment curdled in his belly.

Why couldn't she see that his words were prompted by deep, genuine emotion? Somehow Shelley had slipped under his guard, without his knowing his feelings for her had grown into something that felt suspiciously like love. Perhaps it was because they'd worked so closely together that their relationship had skipped over most of the introductory steps. Whatever the reason, he admitted he could no longer deny what he felt for her.

Maybe she didn't feel the same way, and, therefore, it hadn't even occurred to her. That left a bad taste in his mouth.

That she'd been so betrayed by a man who had at one time been more than a friend wasn't something she was likely to forget. She had looked to Caleb to prove that he believed in her, accepted her for who and what she was. He'd allowed himself to be blinded by his anger, when he should have understood that she'd been sharing an important part of herself.

He'd botched it but good.

That wasn't the only reason for his foul mood, though. Like most warriors, he wasn't comfortable with periods of inaction. He never felt more alive than when he was planning a mission and carrying it out. His intellect came to life, he saw things with a heightened awareness. His blood thrummed when things came together, like the parts of a machine all working together.

He also knew that things could go south in a heartbeat.

Being left behind was anathema to him, and knowing that Shelley was putting herself in the path of danger only intensified his feelings. His heart felt fractured, but he wouldn't surrender now. Couldn't.

Caleb slammed a fist into an open palm. At the sound, Tommy looked up. Was there a question in his eyes? Caleb couldn't tell.

"I'm sorry if I scared you, buddy," he murmured, pulling Tommy to him and gathering him close. "It's all right."

But it wasn't. He felt it.

Anger carried Shelley through the drive to Ramiherison's town house. More than anger, though, was disappointment.

She knew his protectiveness was prompted by caring, but that didn't excuse his dictatorial manner. Hadn't she been through that with Jeffrey?

Not again.

It was hard, brutally hard, to focus on the job with her senses scrambled from when he'd drawn her into his arms. It hadn't helped when he'd told her *You matter to me.*

It hadn't helped at all.

In Caleb's arms, she'd felt safe, protected. It was a foreign feeling, and oddly frightening, to realize how easily she could give over control and simply rely on his strength, but that wasn't who she was. It never would be.

She did her best to push all that from her mind and concentrate fully on the mission.

Ramiherison's town house wasn't overly large, but its location was a good one. Nicer, Shelley wondered, than what a marshal's salary warranted? She knocked, and, to her surprise, felt the door give. She pushed it open, waited.

Would a law enforcement officer leave a door unlocked, much less open? Shelley withdrew her weapon, kept it at her side.

"Marshal? Marshal Ramiherison?" When no one answered, she walked through a formal living room, noting the expensive appointments. Though tasteful enough, she supposed, the effect was too ornate for her liking, the jewel and pastel tones competing with each other.

A short hallway led to what appeared to be a great room combined with the kitchen. The air held an unnatural stillness, a second warning that something wasn't right. A chill peppered her skin.

There.

A woman's legs extended from behind a leather sofa.

Shelley walked around the sofa, stared at the face and recognized the woman immediately from her picture. Victoria Ramiherison. Dark hair was matted with blood. Shelley moved the hair back to see two small, neat bullet holes in the forehead.

As murders went, it wasn't the worst she'd ever seen. Not by far. She'd been in some field of law enforcement or another for most of her adult life and had seen firsthand that people's cruelty to one another knew no limits.

The fact that viewing a dead body still disturbed her despite the self-protective layers she'd had to construct to retain her sanity was both a blessing and a curse. When the sight of a wasted life, even that of a cop who was probably dirty, didn't bother her, she'd know it was time to get out and do something else.

She knelt and felt the woman's neck. Judging from the warmth of the body, she hadn't been dead for long. Warily, Shelley looked about. The murderer could still be there.

Slowly, she got to her feet, backed up a foot. Two. She would let herself out, report the murder to the Marshals' office and get back to Caleb and Tommy. Caleb needed to know what was going on.

Fear grabbed her like a cold hand at the back of her neck, and she sensed a sudden darkness in the air. A prickly sensation crawled up her spine.

Though she kept perfectly still, her body readied for action, adrenaline pouring through her, sending her senses into overdrive. She kept her hands loose, even as they wanted to squeeze into fists. One by one, the hairs on the back of her neck lifted. Her nerves were jangling like an armful of bracelets.

The faint sound of something clicking on the floor caught her attention. Before she could fully register it, a whisper of movement stirred the air. She whirled, but it was too late.

The blow came swiftly.

Sudden pain stole her breath. Black-and-silver spiderwebs flashed across her vision.

Shelley felt herself floating to the oblivion that beckoned her. She had to fight it, but her mind refused to cooperate. Unwillingly, she felt herself being dragged along into the soft allure of unconsciousness.

THIRTEEN

Minutes became hours, and Shelley hadn't returned. Caleb checked his watch for what seemed the hundredth time. There was no way checking out Ramiherison could have taken this long.

Worry was swallowing him whole, and he didn't know how to fight it. A sense of quiet desperation squeezed around his heart. At the same time, fear hit like a fist and forced its way down his throat. He felt as though he were being clawed apart by the raw power of it.

Caleb clenched his fists at his sides. *Where was she?*

He felt alone all the way to his soul, and then he realized that he wasn't alone at all.

"Lord, what do I do?"

His plea went unanswered. Or maybe his heart was too hardened to hear the Lord's words. He didn't know.

As the sky darkened, Caleb helped Tommy get ready for bed.

The youngster's eyes seemed to plead with Caleb to do something. But what could he do? All of his attempts to reach his nephew had met with failure. Never had he felt so helpless.

"What is it? Talk to me. Please." The words stuck in his throat. Tommy remained as silent as ever.

Caleb put the bear that Tommy was never without into the boy's arms. "Your friend's right here." He pressed a kiss to Tommy's forehead.

With a tiny sigh, Tommy slid into sleep.

Caleb resumed his prayer, begging for the Lord's guidance. "Shelley's missing, and Tommy is in so much pain that it's tearing us both apart. More than ever, I need You."

Head bowed, Caleb continued to pray, this time in silence. It was at that moment that he noticed that a section of the stitching around the bear's neck didn't appear to match the rest of it.

He eased the bear from Tommy's arms. The stuffed animal had taken its share of abuse, one ear torn, the fur scruffy, as though it had been washed many times, but none of that held Caleb's interest.

He examined the stitching more closely. He'd been right. The thread was slightly different in one portion. He withdrew his pocket knife, carefully undid the stitches, then probed that area, his fingers closing around a small object. A USB drive.

In that instant, Caleb knew why someone wanted to kidnap Tommy.

Michael must have put crucial information on the drive and then hidden it in the bear. His message to Caleb finally made sense. *Bear with me.*

"It took me a while, but I finally figured it out," Caleb mused aloud.

He headed to the kitchen, plugged the drive in the computer Shelley had retrieved from her office, and waited for the laptop to boot up. When it did, he saw that the drive contained only one file. He opened the document. At first, it appeared to be only columns of figures and dates. After a few minutes' study, he began to understand what he was reading.

Payoffs to police, the mayor's office, all the way up to the state legislature were noted. Dollar amounts of drugs and dates that they were moved. Okay. That made sense. Jeremy Saba, the man Michael had been prosecuting, dealt in drugs, among other things. But it wasn't Saba that Michael had named as the boss of the biggest crime organization in the East Coast. Saba was barely a footnote.

With every word Caleb read, his anger festered, and a low guttural sound crawled up his throat.

Shelley awoke slowly. Her head felt as if it was exploding in pain, causing every muscle of her body to tighten against it. The appeal of the dark place where she'd floated in and out of consciousness called to her, but she resisted its lure.

She couldn't outwit her captor if she succumbed to it, so she willed her mind to clear, to rid itself of the heavy-headedness that persisted in fuzzing her thinking. When she tried to move, she discovered she was bound to a metal pipe that supported the ceiling.

Cautiously, she attempted to lift her head from where it sagged against her shoulder and quickly discovered that the slightest movement sent piercing darts to her brain. Dizziness and nausea vied to see which would win. Okay, so she wouldn't be doing any gymnastics in the near future.

Ironically, the pain banished the last of her confusion.

A scurrying sound had Shelley peering in the near darkness. Though she could see very little, she had the impression of size. Damp and cold seeped into her, and she shivered.

She wasn't afraid of rats, but neither did she relish having one crawl over her. A shudder raced through her. She wasn't claustrophobic. Not exactly. But she'd had a fear of dark, enclosed spaces ever since her mother had locked her in the storage unit so many years ago, a fear reinforced by the teenage boys tying her up in a basement.

Despite years of training, a thin layer of terror descended over her.

Over time she'd worked hard to rid herself of that fear, seeing it as a handicap. She'd discovered you could handle your fear in two different ways. Bury your head in the sand or do something about it. She'd chosen the latter. Now she concentrated on her breathing in an attempt to calm her runaway thoughts.

In.

Out.

In.

Out.

Gradually, her anxiety subsided, and she was able to think rationally. She pushed away her fear. She needed to marshal all of her resources if she were to free herself.

She listened for any sound from the outside that might give a clue as to where she was. Only the rustling of the wind in the trees gave any hint. That hardly narrowed it down. Atlanta was a city of trees.

Shelley reminded herself that she was a professional. She'd been in tight situations in the past. This was no different.

Find the opening and make her move.

Only there was no opening.

With her arms bound behind her back and her feet tethered as well, she was totally immobile. That didn't mean she was beaten. Far from it.

Carefully, she twisted her head to one side, hoping to ease the kink in her neck. It brought a modicum of relief. Moreover, she didn't feel the need to retch with the effort.

Arms and legs cramped to the point of pain, but she wouldn't allow her current predicament to defeat her. She had never quit on herself. More important, the Lord had never quit on her.

She started shifting from side to side once more. Her movements caused the ropes to loosen. If only she could pull the pipe from the brackets holding it in place, she could slip the ropes from her wrists. Sweat trickled down the back of her neck, like ants attempting to crawl beneath her skin. She ignored it and kept working.

A lurch of excitement coursed through her. Did the pipe give? Just a little? She rocked back and forth again.

It definitely moved.

Over and over, she rocked, first one way, then the opposite. The ropes chafed her skin until a warm stickiness coated her hands. She ignored the blood, the pain, and concentrated on her goal. Her progress was agonizingly slow, but she refused to give up.

A dull throb spiked under Shelley's scalp where her head had landed against the pipe. Blood trickled down the side of her face. Sweat prickled her skin, making it itch.

Ignore it.

Focus on freeing yourself.

The ropes started to give. Just a little, but enough to encourage her to keep trying. Beneath the shirt that clung to her skin, her shoulders squared. She'd use what she had: faith and tenacity.

Her wrists were now freely bleeding, and weariness dogged at her when the pipe gave another inch. Anticipation, fueled by determination, had her adrenaline pumping, lending her extra strength. One of the ropes broke.

Almost free.

Tears of frustration turned into ones of joy. She'd done it.

Caleb read Michael's words, a growing fury filling his heart.

I should have seen it years before. I was blind. I'm sorry, bro. I really messed up. If you're reading this, it means the worst has happened. Take care of Tommy. I love you.

Alfred Kruise was dirty. He wasn't just on the take. He had organized the entire operation and used his position as federal prosecutor to sabotage any attempts at taking down those who carried out his bidding.

Caleb gripped the edge of the desk as a wave of nausea rolled through him. He felt dizzy with it. All the while that Michael had worked for Kruise, the older man was betraying him and every other honest person in the prosecutor's office.

"I'll finish this," Caleb promised his brother. "Count on it."

He went over the document again, reading more carefully this time, astounded at all the evidence Michael had accumulated. No wonder Kruise wanted to get his hands on the drive. It would bury him.

Caleb was enraged at Kruise's betrayal. His brother had always regarded Kruise as a mentor, a friend.

The invitation to stay in the Kruises' guesthouse now took on a sinister meaning. Kruise had set Caleb up for the gunman. Then Kruise had changed his mind, and his men had tried to take Tommy. A fresh wave of rage roiled through Caleb as he thought of Kruise and his thugs terrorizing a seven-year-old boy.

Another thought occurred to him. He picked up the phone and called a buddy in the Pentagon's records division. A few minutes of conversation netted Caleb the link he was looking for.

His thoughts hopscotched to Shelley. A new dread filled him as he thought of her delay. What if she'd stumbled across something at Ramiherison's apartment to point her to Kruise?

There was no reason to think that Shelley had gone to the Kruise estate, but Caleb couldn't get past the idea that somehow she'd found the link between Kruise and Ramiherison. She wouldn't back down when faced with danger. Fear and guilt congealed in his heart. If not for him, Shelley would probably not have placed herself in the cross fire.

A noise on the stairway snagged her attention, and the overhead light went on. She did her best to replace the ropes and then slumped against the pipe, feigning unconsciousness.

Her captor sauntered over. "I know you're awake, sweetheart. And I knew what you were up to. Thought I'd give you just enough time to think you could escape."

She didn't respond. The voice was an unfamiliar one.

He tapped her cheek. "Not going to talk, eh? Too bad. I'm sure I would enjoy talking with such a lovely woman."

Now was her chance. She head-butted him in the face, knocking him off balance. The crack of bone told her she'd most likely broken his nose.

Her assailant staggered backward. She took advantage of the seconds when he was off balance and, throwing all her force into her elbow, caught him on the side of the temple.

With one arm literally tied behind her back, she was at a distinct disadvantage. The stunned look in the man's eyes told her she'd gotten in a good blow and done some damage. In the few seconds it took for him to recover, she quickly freed her other hand.

Needles of pain shot up her arm.

He let out a war cry and clamped his hands around her neck. She pushed up on his arms with her arm, breaking his hold, a self-defense trick she'd picked up at the police academy. She pressed her advantage and pummeled him with her fist.

Pure rage sparked his eyes.

Shelley pivoted, settling her weight on her left foot, and launched a kick to his right knee. She registered a quick flash of her captor's fists and feet, the slap of flesh striking flesh, the grunts as blows landed.

After her enforced inactivity, though, the punch lacked its customary power, and the swell of lactic acid in her muscles made her dizzy. Still, she managed to inflict some more damage.

He groaned but still managed to grab hold of her hair, yanking it unmercifully. She couldn't break his grip. Tears stung her eyes as he tightened his hold.

She fought with everything she had, but her reserves were severely depleted. Her body wouldn't pony up any more energy.

With his left hand still tangled in her hair, he slapped her with the right. She wanted to tell him that he fought like a girl, but couldn't get the words out because blood was quickly filling her mouth. Panting, fighting back nausea, she worked to free herself, but his hold was too strong.

She gasped for a breath in a throat that was cottony, but the sound came out in a raspy wheeze, broken and thin. She couldn't hold out anymore and fell against him but not until she'd grabbed hold of the loose metal button hanging from his jacket, praying he wouldn't notice.

The feral gleam in his eyes was a match to the fist that slammed against her jaw with the force of a sledgehammer.

Pain sang along her jaw where his fist had connected. More blood trickled down her face, onto her neck. The coppery smell of it made her want to gag, but she took satisfaction in gazing at his ruined nose.

Without releasing his hold on her, he dragged her to a wooden chair.

With ruthless efficiency, he bound her to the chair at the upper arms, wrists and at each ankle. She bent her arms, trying to put as much space as possible between them and the arms of the chair, but all she bought for her efforts was a measly quarter of an inch.

His sour breathing spilling in her face, he glared down at her, face marred by the blow she'd struck to his nose. Blood coated his lips, and he swiped at it. "I wish I had time right now to give you what you deserve."

Shelley kept her expression impassive, but inwardly, she shuddered. Her skin bristled with goose bumps, the dread of her captor's words working into her mind. She reminded herself to believe. She only had to hold on until Caleb found her.

A surge of raw emotion welled up inside her. Would he know that she loved him, despite the angry words they'd hurled at each other? She hoped so. She knew Caleb wouldn't rest until he'd rescued her. The thought gave her a measure of hope until she realized he had no idea where she was.

With a final, cruel laugh, her captor left.

Shelley refused to give way to the current of panic that threatened. Instead she called upon thousands of hours of training and forced herself into cool detached professionalism. Fear wouldn't get her out of this alive. Training and intelligence would, plus a whole lot of faith.

Though her hands were tied behind her back, she was *not* helpless and began to pray. Trusting both God and Caleb was all Shelley could do right now.

The Lord would hear her prayers, even those not uttered aloud. He knew what was in her heart, what her needs were. She prayed regularly and went to church whenever she could, but had she ever truly placed herself in God's hands and trusted that He would make everything right?

Now she prayed with real intent, begging for His protection and care, for herself, for Caleb and Tommy. *I can't do it on my own, Lord. I need You.*

FOURTEEN

Caleb punched in Salvatore Santonni's number. "I need a favor. Can I leave Tommy with you?"

At Sal's agreement, Caleb got directions. Before he left Shelley's house, he went to her desk, found another USB drive and tucked it in the zippered pocket of his cargo pants. He took the drive he'd found hidden in the bear and placed it in the desk with other office supplies, then bundled Tommy in the car and drove to Sal's place.

"What's the sit rep?" the former Delta asked.

At any other time, Caleb would have smiled at Sal's shorthand for situation report. He gave a rundown of what he'd found on the drive. "I've got to find Shelley before she connects the dots and decides to go up against Kruise herself."

Sal rubbed his jaw with his knuckles. "She's got too much savvy to take him on all by her lonesome, but could be that she didn't have a choice. If what you're saying about Kruise is true, he's got police and marshals and more in his pocket." Sal's expression turned grim. "Means we don't know who to trust."

Caleb clasped the man's shoulder. "I don't know how to thank you."

"Thanks don't belong between brothers."

The reference to the Delta brotherhood gave Caleb a shot of much-needed hope. "I'll let you know when I find her. Meanwhile, keep Tommy safe."

Caleb drove to Ramiherison's house only to find cops and marshals swarming around it, along with a news van and the reporter Shelley had pointed out.

A light rain blurred the blue-and-red flashing lights bouncing across the asphalt road. There was no sign of the vehicle Shelley had been driving. "What's going on?" he asked a cop.

The officer stiffened. "Nothing that concerns you."

Caleb decided a little honesty was in order. "Look, I'm Michael Judd's brother. I'm looking into his murder. The lady marshal was one of his protection detail."

The policeman relaxed a fraction. "I'm real sorry about that. I didn't know your brother personally, but he was one of the good ones."

"Can you tell me what happened?"

"Someone murdered the marshal." The stark words were delivered with a grimness that Caleb recognized. Law enforcement officers tended to close ranks when one of their own was killed.

"How?"

"Double tap to the forehead."

Two shots to the forehead probably meant a pro had taken her out. "Anyone else hurt?"

"No one else there." The man raised a brow. "You know something the authorities should?"

Caleb weighed his response, uncertain where the officer's loyalties lay. He couldn't afford to trust the wrong person. Not after what had happened to Matheson and now Ramiherison. Though the man appeared to be aboveboard, he could be on Kruise's payroll. "Thanks for your time."

Caleb got back in the car.

He made the drive to the Kruise estate, his mind churning with the latest development. It was obvious that Kruise and those working for him were tying up loose ends.

Caleb did a surveillance of the house and grounds. The rain had picked up, gurgling in gutters and along the curb. There was no sign of Shelley's car, but that didn't mean Kruise and his goons didn't have her.

The security system at the Kruise estate was state-of-the-art, but it had one very big flaw: everything was dependent upon the central power system. If it were disengaged, the entire system shut down.

His Delta training had taught him how to disarm most security systems. The skill came in handy now as he shut down the controller and entered through the French doors at the garden, gun at his side.

He found Kruise in a richly paneled library. Sitting behind a lake-sized desk polished to a high sheen, the man looked every inch the southern gentleman in his lightweight silk suit and patterned tie.

Kruise didn't look surprised to see him. "I've been waiting for you. I knew it was only a matter of time before you figured it out. Just like Michael." Kruise shook his head. "I tried to warn Michael. I tried to warn you, too, even when I was sure you wouldn't walk away."

"The newspaper clipping," Caleb said through clenched teeth. "You sent it." Everything was beginning to make sense. Michael, who had looked up to Kruise for years, must have told him what had happened to Ethan. "You had Michael and Grace killed. Maybe even did it yourself."

The older man didn't appear fazed by the accusation.

"You're the head of the crime syndicate, the one that Michael called the linchpin. What I want to know is why. You have all the money you could ever want."

"Power," Kruise said with a theatrical gesture. "Power makes the world go round. It's what makes the difference between the haves and the have-nots. The rich and the poor. It's the ultimate drug."

Caleb resisted the urge to reach across the desk, bunch the man's expensive shirt in his hands and shake the living daylights out of him. For the first time in his life, Caleb understood the meaning of the phrase "drunk with power." That was clearly Kruise's drug of choice.

No one had seen the evil beneath the polished surface that Kruise presented to the world. No one except Michael. Michael had seen it, and it had cost him his life.

"For years, I watched the criminals run circles around law enforcement," Kruise said. "I finally decided I could do it better. If I do say so myself, I run an efficient operation. No one moves drugs through the Eastern Corridor like I do."

"Do you ever think about the lives you ruin with your drugs? Innocent children trapped in a life of addiction."

"If they were so innocent, they wouldn't have taken the drugs in the first place."

"You've got an answer for everything, don't you?" Caleb asked, fingers tightening around the butt of the gun.

The federal prosecutor skimmed his fingers down his custom-tailored jacket. "Of course. How do you think I got where I am?"

"By killing a man who thought of you as a friend."

"Don't be naive. But that's the trouble with you Judd brothers, isn't it? Your refusal to see the world as it really is." His expression was about as condescending and smug as a face could get.

"How you see it, you mean?" Caleb taunted. "Everything has a price. Loyalty. Friendship. Integrity."

Kruise snapped his fingers, a gesture of dismissal. "None of that matters. Don't you get it? Power is the only thing that really matters. Money's all fine and good, but it doesn't compare to real power. Power to make people do what I say. Important people. Governors. Senators. Reporters. Someday I'll be putting my hat in the ring for the White House. I already have key players in place."

Caleb shuddered at the idea of Kruise in the nation's highest office. "You're very sure of yourself."

"Why not? Your brother was the only thing standing in my way. With him gone, there's no one to stop me."

Kruise propped his elbows on the desk and tented his fingers. "Michael was a fool. Everything was right in front of him, but he didn't see it until it was too late. It was embarrassingly easy to pull the wool over his eyes. He worshipped the ground I walked on. Even at the end, he thought he could talk me into giving myself up." He scoffed. "Your brother had this idea he could explain that what I was doing was wrong and that I would have a change of heart."

Kruise said the words with a kind of disdain that had Caleb struggling to control his rage. That was Michael, always trying to give someone a second chance.

"Did you know he begged me not to kill his sweet little Grace? Actually begged. As if it would make a difference. It was disgusting, hearing a grown man beg. But I have to hand it to him. He never begged for himself."

Breathe, Caleb told himself. Kruise was trying to make him angry, to use that against him. Anger was a weakness.

"Enough," Caleb snapped, unable to hear another word about his brother.

"It really is too bad about your brother," Kruise said in a musing tone. "He could have gone far. Almost as far as I have.

"Don't you love modern technology?" He tapped a button, and a bank of screens appeared. Each screen held a different picture, the city broken down by geographical segments.

"It's called domain awareness," he continued, gesturing to the screens. "Anytime some of our fine boys in blue were ready to stage a raid, I knew, practically before they did. Occasionally, I'd let a small bust go through. Give them a bone."

Caleb longed to smash his fist in Kruise's smug face, but he resisted. "What about Saba?"

"Saba?" Kruise barked out a laugh. "He's a puppet. He doesn't have the brains to run a lemonade stand, much less a criminal empire. But he had the look. You know—smooth, handsome in a slick kind of way. Just like you'd expect a crime lord to look. All he has to do is look the part. He gets his take. That's all he cares about."

"And all the while it was you running the whole operation. Drugs. Money laundering. Counterfeiting." Caleb didn't bother keeping the disgust from his voice.

"If worse comes to worst, Saba will take the fall. All the paperwork, all the bank accounts, are in his name."

"You thought of everything. Except Michael."

"Michael was a disappointment," Kruise continued with irritating calm. "I'd groomed him from the beginning. Gave him the most plum jobs. Made sure he was seen at the right places with the right people. He could have gone far." Kruise shook his head in regret. "Much as I want to believe that I can live forever, I knew the time would come when I'd have to turn over the torch."

"Michael was supposed to have been your heir apparent."

Kruise beamed at Caleb, a benevolent teacher bestowing an accolade on a rather slow student who had finally come up with the right answer. "You see it, don't you? Michael had everything. The right look, the right wife, the right connections. He could have had it all."

He saw it, Caleb thought. And it made him sick. As it must have turned Michael's stomach as well when he learned that his mentor, the godfather of his child, had been grooming him to take over the largest crime organization on the Eastern Coast.

Caleb absorbed that. "Tommy saw you there. He saw you kill Michael and Grace."

"Michael had become a problem. I never intended to kill Grace, but she walked in at an inopportune time. Collateral damage."

"Why didn't you kill Tommy?" Caleb asked the question, though he was pretty sure he knew the answer.

"I knew Michael had the goods on me somewhere. Afterward, I realized he must have given the kid something," Kruise said, confirming Caleb's guess. "The little brat ran and hid before we could get to him."

"And after you found the drive? What were you going to do with Tommy?"

"What do you think?"

"You'd kill a child?" Stupid question, Caleb

told himself. Kruise had already made it clear he'd do anything to protect his empire.

"I can't take the chance that he's going to start talking about what he saw. I've done worse." There was no remorse in his voice. If anything, it was pride Caleb heard. "Far worse." A nasty smile crept from one side of his jaw to the other, accompanied by a vile laugh.

Caleb didn't bother to hide his revulsion. "The drive makes for some very interesting reading. Turns out that my brother has a real flair for writing down dates and amounts."

He didn't give Kruise a chance to reply. "You're done, Al. You and your whole operation are going down. I'm going to take special pleasure in seeing you put away for life."

"Oh, I hardly think so. Once you and that little private detective you hired are out of the way, I'm untouchable."

Shelley.

"What have you done with her? If you've hurt her…"

"She's all right. For now." Kruise steepled his fingers together again. "I did some digging on your bodyguard. She's a bulldozer. She never gives up, never gives in. And she never walks away. I knew we'd have to deal with her, sooner or later." He made a tsking sound.

Caleb had to hand it to Kruise. He had Shelley, with her gritty brand of courage, pegged.

What made her so good at her job also made her a problem to be eliminated.

"It's too bad, because she could have been an asset. It would have been amusing to see if I could turn her." Kruise laughed. "Not that I could, of course. She's too much of a straight arrow, but the process of trying would have been entertaining."

"Where is Shelley?" Caleb demanded, fear for her congealing in his heart.

Kruise bestowed a considering look upon Caleb. "Do you know that you're even a bigger fool than your brother? Do you think you can take me down? Think again, soldier boy."

"Oh, I'm thinking all right. I'm thinking of how you're going to look in prison orange." Caleb raised his voice. "Come on out, Amachker. I know you're there."

After a long moment, Grant Amachker stepped out from behind a bifold door, a gun in his hand. The marshal's nose was bandaged.

At a guess, Caleb figured the man's nose had run in to Shelley. Any satisfaction he felt at that was quickly tempered by worry for her. What had they done to her? Seeing Amachker's condition only intensified Caleb's fear for the woman who had come to mean everything to him.

"You couldn't have known," Amachker challenged.

"No? Only two people knew I was looking at

Victoria Ramiherison. One of them, I trust with my life. The other was you.

"And then there was something else."

"What?" Amachker asked.

"I did some checking. You and Kruise served together in the First Gulf War. He was a captain. You were a master sergeant."

"Yeah? That doesn't prove anything. Thousands of us were over there."

"But you were in the same platoon. And one more thing... The two of you played ball together at Georgia Tech."

"Still not proof," the marshal said, but his voice lacked conviction this time.

"I think when the *real* lawmen look into your finances, they'll find all the proof they need."

"I should have killed him that first night," Amachker hissed to Kruise, resentment souring his voice. "But you called it off."

"As I explained," Kruise said with weary patience, "we needed him to help us find the USB drive. And he did."

The last piece fell into place. Caleb had wondered why the assailant who'd broken into the guesthouse hadn't killed him, why he'd suddenly taken off.

"It was you."

"Got it in one." Amachker turned on Kruise. "It's your fault we had to kill Ramiherison. If you'd let me take care of Judd like I wanted to that night, Victoria would still be alive."

"She was a weak link. Besides, she makes the perfect scapegoat. All the evidence will point to her as the mole. The murders of Michael and Grace Judd are avenged, and business will resume as usual."

"Business as usual?" Caleb snarled. "Is that what they're calling murder these days?"

"Murder has been a business ever since Cain killed Abel."

"Is that how you excuse it?"

"I don't have to excuse it. It's a fact of life." Kruise sounded bored with the conversation.

"Quit yammering," Amachker said, taking a step in Caleb's direction. "We've got business to take care of." He laughed at his own joke.

"From all reports, you were a good cop, doing a good job," Caleb challenged.

Amachker's motivations for going into cahoots with Kruise were obvious. He'd probably gotten tired of seeing the fat cats get richer.

Amachker gestured to Kruise. "He offered me ten times the government pension just for a few jobs. Not bad. Not bad at all. And that was only the beginning." His lips stretched into a nasty leer while his brows flattened into one hard line.

"You're more of a fool than I thought," Caleb said, "if you think he's going to let you live. You're expendable. Just like Ramiherison."

Amachker stopped, turned to face Kruise. "What about it?"

"He's lying." For the first time Kruise looked annoyed. "It's the oldest trick in the book. He's trying to turn us against each other."

"I'm the one with the gun and it's aimed at you, Al." Caleb took pleasure in the man's thinned lips at the abbreviated name. "Now tell your buddy to drop his weapon and maybe both of you will walk out of here alive."

"Do you play chess?" Kruise asked.

Caleb was nonplussed at the question. "A little."

"Then you'll know that a player never underestimates his opponent's queen."

The queen. Irene Kruise? The thought hadn't fully formed before Caleb was zapped with thousands of volts of electricity.

Pain and shock raced through his body as he crumpled to the floor. Blackness seeped in from the corners of his vision until there was nothing.

FIFTEEN

"Brought you some company." Amachker threw Caleb down on a concrete floor.

Caleb was aware enough to know that he was in a basement. He knew his gaze was unfocused, his jaw slack. He wondered who Amachker was talking to.

When he saw Shelley, he nearly groaned. Some hero he'd turned out to be. All he'd managed to do was to get himself captured. He blinked in an effort to clear his vision and looked more closely at her. Dried blood had crusted at the corners of her mouth, and fresh rage swelled inside of him.

"You'll pay for what you've done to her," he croaked, hearing his voice as if from a distance.

"What? In your condition? Hardly." Scoffing, the marshal turned to Shelley. "Your rescuer isn't looking so great after all, is he?" He undid the ropes binding her to a chair and shoved her to the ground. Ruthlessly, he tied her and Caleb back to back to a pole, denying them even the comfort of looking at each other.

"You won't feel quite so clever when you're behind bars," she retorted.

Out of the corner of his eye, Caleb caught the movement of Amachker's arm as he raised it. "Leave her alone," he growled, his words still slurred.

Amachker backed off, not following through with the threat.

Caleb understood that neither he nor Shelley were expected to walk out of the basement. Amachker and Kruise obviously didn't care if Caleb and Shelley could identify them. Nor did they anticipate either Shelley or Caleb sitting in a witness box to testify against them.

"We've never been formally introduced," the marshal said to Shelley. "Grant Amachker, US marshal at your service." He started to offer his hand, then withdrew it. "Sorry. I can see that you're all tied up." He snickered at his own joke.

"A dirty cop," she sneered. "You're nothing but a cliché."

"I've been called a lot worse by a lot better than you."

"Don't waste your breath, Amachker. They're not worth the effort." The big man himself had ventured to the basement. In his hand was the USB drive Caleb had put in his pocket earlier.

Caleb lifted his head enough to see a woman standing next to Kruise. Irene Kruise.

"You've caused us a lot of trouble," she said, and her lips pinched at the corners with regal disdain. "You and your bodyguard. Too bad you didn't pay attention to the warnings."

"Don't be a fool, Irene." Kruise's voice held the snap of a whip. "A man like Judd doesn't walk away." He held up the USB drive. "I knew you'd have it on you. You wouldn't leave it just anywhere. Now I have it."

"We gave him the chance," Irene said, sounding as though the whole thing was Caleb's fault. "Just like we did Michael. It's too bad that stupidity seems to run in the family."

Caleb strained against the ropes binding him to the pole. Desperation churned through him. Seated on a concrete floor, he felt every muscle in his body protest. "You won't get away with this. Others know the truth."

Kruise kicked Caleb in the ribs with the toe of a highly polished shoe. "Can't you do any better than that?" He turned to Irene. "Come, darling. We'll leave these two in the capable hands of the good marshal and his helper. We've got one more Judd to take care of, and then we're home free."

Tommy. Never had Caleb felt more helpless.

"Amachker," Kruise said. "I don't want a mess left down here. Go up to the garage and get some tarps before you take care of them."

"Are you all right?" Caleb asked Shelley after Amachker and the Kruises disappeared up the stairs. They had only a few minutes before Amachker returned.

"Yeah. What about you?"

"I'll live," Caleb said, wincing from where he'd taken the blow to the ribs.

"How'd you know to come here?" she asked.

"Tommy's bear." Caleb quickly related the story of finding the USB drive in the bear, then heading to Ramiherison's place to look for her and from there to the Kruise estate. "It was Kruise all along. He's the mastermind."

If it was the last thing he did, Caleb would make sure the Kruises went down for the murder of Michael and Grace.

But protecting Tommy came first.

"I hope you have a plan, because I'm fresh out," he said. He still couldn't make his tongue work properly.

"As a matter of fact, I do. Here's what we're going to do…"

Caleb listened closely and, despite the grim circumstances, grinned.

Shelley screamed. And kept screaming.

"What's going on down there?" Amachker shouted from the top of the stairs.

"He's dead. Judd's dead. I'm tied to a dead

man." She screamed again. "Get him out of here. I can't stand it."

"You're crazy, lady." But Amachker stomped down the stairs.

"Look at him," Shelley said when Amachker came closer. "He's already turning cold. I can feel it. You killed him. Whatever you did to him stopped his heart." She forced tears to her eyes and hoped she hadn't overplayed the role of hysterical woman.

"I didn't kill anyone." The marshal stooped to study Caleb's slack features. "He's just unconscious. Can't you tell the difference between an unconscious man and a dead one?"

"I tell you, he's dead. He made this gurgling sound and then just stopped breathing."

At that moment, Caleb reared back as far as his restraints allowed and slammed his head into Amachker's face, hitting him in his bandaged nose.

Amachker roared and stumbled backward.

Shelley seized the opportunity. She'd already used the shank of the metal button to saw through the ropes binding her. Freed, she now drove her fist into Amachker's gut.

Her blood hummed; adrenaline flowed. She pivoted, settling her weight on her left foot, and launched a kick to his right knee.

The marshal let out a war cry and clamped his hands around her neck. She pushed up on his arms with hers, breaking his hold, a self-defense trick she'd picked up at the police academy years ago. She pressed her advantage and pummeled him with her fists.

Fury darkened his eyes.

She'd been trained well and now called upon every bit of that training. She didn't kid herself; she was fighting for her and Caleb's lives.

The man kicked out and caught her behind the knee. Before she could right herself, she was down. She feigned being injured, and, when Amachker moved in, she bowed her spine and flipped back up into a standing position.

Shelley spun, kicked out again, caught him in the chest cavity. She followed up by striking out with her fist, intending to ram it beneath his nose, but he wrapped an iron-hard arm around her neck and squeezed. She let her body go limp, taking him by surprise, and he let her go.

The commotion had brought another man down the stairs. Caleb had managed to free himself and was now busy with his own quarry.

Shelley darted a worried look his way, knowing he wasn't a 100 percent after being stunned with the Taser, but he was holding his own.

Caleb gave a roundhouse kick to the man's midsection. With a pump of his legs, he sprang back up. Caleb was ready for him, delivering a sharp jab to the assailant's kidneys, followed by a jab to his jaw. The man gave a whoosh of breath but somehow remained standing and sent out a punch of his own.

Shelley noticed that Amachker had a tell before he advanced. He touched his tongue to his upper lip. He probably wasn't even aware of it. She sidestepped the next punch and delivered a one-two-three jab to her opponent's gut.

The marshal grunted.

She grabbed the man's arm and bent it backward, but her strength was no match to his. He flexed his upper arm, the steely tendons throwing off her hold with insulting ease. She landed an uppercut to the chest and was gratified when he staggered a bit.

Knowing that her strength lay in her legs, she dropped to the floor and swung out, catching Amachker off guard. Blood streamed from his already broken nose, dripping onto her shirt.

Out of the corner of her eye, she saw Caleb move in close and give a hard chop to his opponent's neck. With a gurgling sound, the man crumpled to the floor.

She got to her feet, and, after delivering a blow to the marshal's gut, she yanked his arm, whipsawed it around until he collapsed. When he was facedown on the floor, she planted her knee against the base of his spine and pulled his arms behind his back.

Shelley grabbed the ropes, which had bound

her and Caleb. Efficiently, they tied up the marshal and his henchman.

"Don't worry," Caleb told them. "You won't be here long. As soon as we call the police, they'll be over to pick you up and take you to a nice warm cell."

He turned to Shelley. "We have to get to Tommy. If the Kruises took my car, the GPS will take them right to him."

Caleb fished in Amachker's pockets and found the marshal's keys. He and Shelley raced up the stairs and out the door. Caleb climbed in the driver's seat while Shelley rode shotgun. They made the drive to Sal's house in half the time it should have taken.

They crouched beneath the window and saw that Sal was tied to a chair. "Where do you think Tommy is?" Caleb asked.

"The house has two bedrooms in the back. I'm guessing Tommy's in one of them with Irene.

"I'll take the front," Shelley said. "You take the back. We can do this," she added when he scowled, obviously ready to object. "I go in, distract him. You come through the back, find Tommy, get him out."

"What about you?"

"I'll be okay. Don't make me pull rank on you." His eyes darkened in response.

"Don't make me regret this." He pulled her to him, kissed her. "Okay. Let's do this."

Startled from the kiss, Shelley worked to get her bearings. With a deep breath, she cleared her head and reviewed her options, deciding she had her best chance with surprise. She pushed open the front door, hoping the bold act would startle Kruise enough that Caleb could sneak in the back unnoticed and get Tommy out of the line of fire.

"Long time, no see," she said to Kruise.

She spared a glance at Sal and winced when she saw the blood trickling down his forehead. He hadn't gone down without a fight.

"Sorry, boss. They broke a window, threw in a flash bang." He shook his head in self-disgust.

"I can see I should have taken care of you myself, Ms. Rabb." Kruise moved his weapon on her, the gun in his hand deadly as its aim rested on her. "I suppose you've dispatched Marshal Amachker. Saves me the trouble from taking care of him myself. He was always a second-rater. But he had his uses." Contempt edged his words.

"There doesn't have to be any more killing." Though she kept her gaze on Kruise's face, she made sure she could see his hands. Most people thought that eyes told a person's intent, but, in reality, it was the hands. Right now, Kruise's left hand was twitching, the right holding the gun. The gesture told her he was more nervous than he let on.

"Oh, I think we can. All I have to do is take care of you and your friend and no one will be the wiser."

"You've lost your mind." She gave him a considering look. "But that isn't surprising. I told Amachker he was a cliché, but you're the real cliché. A man who doesn't have what it takes to succeed in life without cheating."

Kruise's face flushed, and she knew she'd scored a point.

"You're a narcissist and a sociopath. All in all, a poor excuse for a human being." Her deliberate taunts, designed to distract him, were working.

"Shut up." His patrician features contorted in a scarcely controlled rage, his nostrils flaring, his eyes slitted.

"Why don't you put down your gun and try and make me?" She was deliberately baiting him to give Caleb more time to find Tommy.

Caleb let himself in through a back window of an empty bedroom. His boots absorbed the sound as they were designed to as he moved across the room and out to the hallway. A door to a second bedroom was closed. He edged it open, saw Irene standing over Tommy.

Caleb took her by surprise and knocked her out, hitting a woman for the first time in his life. He had no choice, not if he were to save Tommy. Swiftly he unthreaded his belt from its loops and bound her hands. He turned to his nephew. "Are you okay?"

The little boy nodded.

"Let's get you out of here." Caleb slid open the window and lifted Tommy to the ground. "Stay there. Don't move. No matter what."

Caleb retraced his steps, this time heading to the living room. He heard Shelley's taunt and knew that Kruise wouldn't be able to resist it. He tucked his gun at the small of his back in the waistband of his jeans, then pulled his shirt over it.

Kruise had raised his weapon, and Shelley was staring him down. Caleb winced; the woman knew no fear.

"You're a coward," she said. "It shows all over you. I have to hand it to you, though. You managed to fool a lot of people for a long time. One thing has me curious."

"What's that?"

"When did you decide to become a murderer?"

An ugly expression crossed Kruise's face. "Enough talk." He waved the gun at her. "Get over here."

She shook her head. "Not going to happen."

"No?" Kruise put his gun against Sal's forehead.

"Don't hurt him. Just...don't." She walked toward Kruise. When she was within reach, he yanked her to him, pressed the gun to her head.

"Judd. I know you're there," Kruise said. "Your pretty bodyguard just got up close and personal with my gun. Things are going to get a lot more personal if you don't get in here in the next three seconds."

Caleb walked into the room, hands up. "You've got me. Let them go."

"I don't think so. I suppose you've already taken care of Irene. She never could do anything right."

Caleb pretended to cower under the threat of Kruise's gun, then plowed into the man in a controlled forward roll, at the same time, making sure he pushed Shelley out of the way. The two men wrestled for the pistol in Kruise's hand.

A shot went off.

At first, Caleb wasn't certain who had been hit. But then he was falling. He heard Shelley's scream. He supposed the bullet must have found its mark, but he didn't feel anything after the initial pain. Breathing was an effort.

A blur of colors and voices passed over him, but he registered only a fraction of them. He needed to tell Shelley something, needed...

But oblivion claimed him.

SIXTEEN

Shelley grabbed the gun and slammed it against Kruise's temple. With him out of commission, she undid the ropes binding Sal to the chair, then tore off her jacket and pressed it against Caleb's chest.

"Call 911." Who was that screaming? Was it her? She didn't recognize her voice. She only knew that Caleb was unconscious and bleeding out in front of her. Her jacket was already soaked with blood. His blood.

All the color had leached from his face, leaving the strong lines and angles oddly slack. *No. No!* The wound continued to bleed profusely. She kept the pressure up even as she felt him slipping away.

From the corner of her eye, she saw Sal tie Kruise to the same chair Sal had been bound to only minutes ago.

The operative knelt beside her. Together, they

performed CPR. "He's breathing," Sal said. "The paramedics will be here in a minute."

As though proving his point, flashing lights appeared at the window. Two paramedics followed upon the heels of four policemen who burst through the door.

Shelley barely registered Sal filling in the police on the Kruises. She was too busy willing the blood to stop flowing from Caleb's body. Her heart seemed to stop, the air trapped in her lungs. She scarcely noticed until she found herself out of breath, as though she'd been running a great distance.

Strong hands set her aside. "Single GSW," the paramedic said.

His partner began intubation. "Got it."

When she tried to reach for Caleb again, Sal held her back. "Let them do their job."

They worked on Caleb, then lifted him onto a gurney, and started toward the ambulance.

She wrenched herself free from Sal and ran to keep up the paramedics. "I'm going with you."

"Sorry, ma'am, but that's against regulations."

She ignored that and climbed into the ambulance, all her energies focused on Caleb. "Caleb Judd. You listen to me. God has a plan for you. And it doesn't include you dying. Not now. Tommy needs you. And I…" Tears clogged her throat. "I need you, too. I love you."

She gripped his hand. "Do you hear that? I love you. Don't you dare die on me."

Did his fingers tighten around hers ever so slightly? She squeezed his in return. Yes! She felt him respond.

"Ma'am, I've got to be able to get to him, and right now you're in my way," one of the paramedics said. "By the way, I think he heard you. I know I did."

Reluctantly, she pulled back, but she couldn't stop the tears from streaming down her cheeks.

They arrived at the hospital, and controlled chaos ensued. Shouts. Hands pushing her aside. Medical personnel swarming around Caleb like bees homing in on a newly opened flower.

"Stay back if you want him to live," a man clad in blue scrubs ordered in a curt voice.

She rounded on him, ready to do battle with anyone who kept her from Caleb. At the last minute, she held her tongue. The doctor was trying to save the life of the man she loved. She stepped back.

"Please…"

The doctor didn't look up. "We'll do our best. That's all I promise. Now get out of my way."

"Thank you."

But the doctor had vanished.

Smells assaulted her senses. Pine cleanser, talc from latex gloves, and antiseptic, combined in an unmistakable smell. Mix in a strong dose of fear and desperation and you had yourself a nasty brew.

She felt her stomach roil against the smells and placed her hands over it in a useless attempt to calm it. It was then she noticed that they were streaked with blood.

She had seen blood before, too much, in her years with Metro PD and then with the Service, but never had the sight of it affected her as it did now. She wiped her hands on the legs of her pants, but it stubbornly remained.

Sal showed up with Tommy. Sal took one look at her face and didn't ask about Caleb. She was grateful because she didn't think she was capable of answering.

"You need to wash up," he said in a low voice.

It was then that she realized that Tommy was staring at the blood on her hands. How stupid could she be?

Sal handed Shelley a bag of clothes. "Figured you could use these."

"Thanks." She retreated to a restroom, did her best to rinse away the blood, and changed out of her soiled clothes.

When she returned, she found Tommy curled up on Sal's lap.

"What happened?" she asked. She hadn't stuck around to see what had happened to the Kruises.

"When I left, Kruise and his wife were claiming that they had been forced to cooperate, that

Amachker was behind the whole thing, and that they were innocent victims." Sal made a sound of disbelief. "The marshals showed up, took them into custody."

A television was on in the background with Taryn Starks reporting on the Kruises' arrest.

"They won't be hurting anyone again," Sal said with satisfaction.

Shelley wished she could believe that, but she didn't make the mistake of underestimating the Kruises. They'd carried out their criminal activities in plain sight for years. They had money and power, a deadly combination. Convicting them wasn't a slam dunk by any means.

Tommy looked up at Shelley. "Uncle Alfred... h-he shot my d-daddy and my m-mommy."

Startled by the sound of Tommy's voice, Shelley knelt down beside him. "You saw Mr. Kruise kill your parents?" She didn't want to make him relive that horror, but she sensed that Tommy had to get the words out.

The boy nodded. "Wh-why did he do that?" Though the words were halting, Tommy was talking. And crying.

"I'm sorry you had to see that, honey," Shelley said softly. "I'm so sorry." She was crying, too, her tears mixing with his.

Tommy didn't say anything more. He yawned widely, snuggled deeper into Sal's arms and closed his eyes.

"He's tuckered," Sal said. "Why don't I take him home with me? I'll make sure he has something to eat, then put him to bed."

"You're a sweetheart."

The big man looked embarrassed. "Don't be spreading that around." He placed a large hand on her shoulder. "Judd's a fighter. He's Delta."

Obviously, for Sal, that said it all. She only prayed it was enough.

Minutes turned into hours, and her prayers bled into one another. What would she do if Caleb didn't make it? No! That wasn't possible. She'd spoken the truth when she told him that God had a plan for him.

When the doctor reappeared two hours later, Shelley held her breath. Blood splattered his scrubs. So much blood.

"Your friend's alive," he said. "Just. The bullet did a lot of damage." The doctor, who looked barely old enough to be out of college, went on to say that the bullet had been a dumdum, tumbling around in the body, nicking organs and causing severe internal bleeding. "Those bullets were designed to inflict as much harm as possible."

Shelley nodded solemnly. She'd seen what dumdums could do. A fellow officer in the Metro PD had taken one to his shoulder during a shootout with some bank robbers. Though he'd lived, he'd never been able to regain full use of his arm and had had to go on disability.

"We had to crack his ribs to get to the bullet," the young doctor continued, "but we got it out. We've got him his stabilized for now. He's healthy, strong, in tip-top shape. That'll work in his favor."

For the first time, something like sympathy appeared in the man's eyes. "There's nothing you can do here."

"I'm not leaving."

"Then I won't waste my time trying to get you to," he said, shaking his head.

"Good."

Shelley continued her vigil in the hospital waiting room and picked at the food Sal had brought. Though her stomach was grumbling with hunger, she didn't have an appetite. How could she eat when she didn't know if Caleb was going to make it? Even if he survived the night, that was no guarantee.

Guilt clung to her like a burr. Caleb had taken a bullet meant for her. It had been her job to protect him, and yet it was he who was fighting for his life. She found the hospital chapel and discovered it empty. After kneeling in front of a pew, she poured out her heart to the Lord.

"Lord, I know You love Caleb, just as You love all Your children. Please save him. Tommy needs him. *I* need him. I don't know what I'll do if he…" She couldn't complete the thought. She didn't know how long she stayed there, continuing to pray, the words now whispered only in her heart, but she knew the Lord heard them.

When she arose, she felt stronger and headed back to the waiting room. She called Sal to check on Tommy, was gratified to hear that he was sleeping, then made a call to the police. The Kruises and Amachker were demanding to see their lawyers and blaming each other.

Any other time, Shelley would have personally followed up, but this wasn't any other time. Caleb was fighting for his life.

Just when she thought she couldn't bear the uncertainty a moment longer, the doctor, looking considerably less fresh than he had hours earlier, returned.

"Your friend is one blessed man. He's in recovery. You can see him in another couple of hours."

Uncaring that she was in the middle of a busy waiting room, she started to weep. "Thank you. Thank you for saving his life."

"I don't know that I had much to do with it. Someone else seemed to be guiding my hands."

The Lord.

"He'll probably sleep through the day," the doctor continued. "Go home, get some rest, then come back."

It was foolish, she supposed, but she couldn't leave. Not yet. Knowing that Caleb was just down the hallway from her allowed her to breathe easier.

When the doctor gave the go-ahead, she'd see him, just to assure herself that he was there, alive. Shelley offered a silent prayer of gratitude to the Lord. He had brought them through this horror.

She knew Caleb and Tommy were going to have a great deal of healing to do over the next weeks and months. It wouldn't be easy. Nothing worthwhile ever was.

She discovered she was hungry, starving, and enthusiastically started in on the sandwich Sal had brought earlier.

Two hours later, a nurse appeared. "You can see Mr. Judd now." Her smile was sympathetic. "Don't worry. He's doing fine."

Shelley murmured her thanks as the nurse showed her to the room. Her heart lurched at the sight of Caleb lying on the hospital bed, so quiet and still, tubes hooked up to his arms, a monitor attached to his chest by wires. An IV stood guard, a skinny sentinel.

He was pale, but his breathing sounded normal. Careful of the tube attached to his hand, she curled her fingers around his. For a fraction of a moment, his eyes opened. "Shelley." The word came out as a croak, but she heard her name.

"I'm here."

A tiny smile clutched at the corners of his

mouth. "Good." But his voice faded, and his eyes closed once more.

Shelley stayed there until the nurse returned. "You can see him later," she promised. "Right now, he needs to rest."

Sal brought Tommy to the hospital that afternoon. Since Tommy wasn't allowed to go in the ICU, Shelley sat with him on the sofa in the waiting room and pulled him to her. "Everything's going to be okay."

Tommy snuggled closer. "Uncle Caleb…is all right?" His words came slowly, tentatively, as though he were testing his voice and himself.

"He will be. In the meantime, you and I will have to take care of each other." She tightened her arms around the little boy.

"Mommy and Daddy…gone."

Shelley tightened her hold. "I know. But you're not alone." No, Tommy wasn't alone. He had Caleb and her and Sal. And, most important, he had the Lord.

Tommy touched her cheek. "Pretty."

For the first time in hours, she smiled. "Thank you."

SEVENTEEN

Caleb was regaining his strength, but the process was agonizingly slow.

Several days ago, he'd woken from a haze of pain-drenched sleep, disoriented as to where he was or what day it was.

"How long?" he'd rasped upon seeing Shelley.

"A week."

A week. Seven days lost. "Tommy?"

"He's with your cousin." Shelley named the woman, a cousin on his father's side. "She read about what happened in the paper and offered to take care of Tommy until you're out of the hospital."

Had she told him that before? He wasn't sure.

Was it possible he'd seen Shelley's face every time he'd opened his eyes? Surely she hadn't stayed here all that time.

His gaze took in the picture she made with her short hair framing her face, so beautiful it made him ache inside.

That had been three days ago. Now that he felt stronger, he wanted to be up and doing something. Impatience chafed at him. More than that, though, was uncertainty. He couldn't put off making a decision about returning to Delta much longer.

He feared leaving the only life he'd known for more than a decade would rip his heart right out of his chest, but he had a responsibility to Tommy. Would the battle between family and duty always wage within him?

"I'm fine," he insisted when Shelley tried to adjust his pillow. He sent her a smile that had nothing in it. Smart as Shelley was, she probably saw the emptiness of the gesture.

"You're not fine. You're only ten days out of surgery."

The longest ten days of his life. Sitting up in his hospital bed was the most vigorous activity he'd performed. A film of sweat broke out across his brow at the least movement, his breathing labored as though he'd just completed a marathon.

"If you'd stop fussing over me, maybe I could get out of this bed and take myself to the bathroom for a change." Having to rely on a nurse for the most personal of needs was torture.

Hurt flickered in Shelley's eyes. He did his best not to notice.

"Okay, tough guy. Let's see you get up and walk across the room."

Careful of the IV line hooked up to his hand, Caleb swung his legs over the side of the bed and pushed himself up. One shaky step was all he managed before collapsing back on the bed.

"One more day," he said on a growl, "and then I'm out of here."

"You'll get up when the doctor tells you that you can get up. In the meantime, behave yourself."

He bit back a smile. His and Shelley's relationship had taken a turn. There was a new ease between them, a familiarity that made him want to take it to the next level, but he wasn't free to do that until he settled some things in his own life. Perhaps it was the uncertainty of the future that had caused him to lash out at her just now.

"Your cousin's bringing Tommy by after school," she said.

"That's good."

Shelley leaned over, her intention obvious.

Caleb turned his head so that her lips grazed his cheek rather than his mouth. From the tiny furrow between her brows, he knew she was puzzled by his behavior. He was puzzled, as well. Why couldn't he find the words to tell her how he felt?

"Shelley." But the name came out more as a sigh.

"I've got to go," she said, keeping her face averted. "I'll be by tomorrow."

"Great." But the word lacked conviction.

Shelley didn't try to kiss him again, and he told himself he was grateful. He couldn't accept her kisses until he knew what he was going to do with his life. She had put her life on the line for him and Tommy again and again. She had a right to expect more from him than sharp words.

When she left, Caleb wanted to call her back, to tell her that he loved her, but something held him back. The time in the ambulance was still fuzzy in his mind. Urgent hands had worked over him, needles poked into him. He'd drifted in and out of consciousness. Had Shelley told him that she loved him? He wasn't sure.

There was still so much uncertainty between them, including the fact that he found himself at a major crossroads in his life.

Shelley reminded herself that Caleb was still recovering. It was no big deal that he had turned away from her. Just because he hadn't wanted her to kiss him didn't mean that he didn't want her. Of course not.

Maybe it was as simple as bad breath, but the lame explanation didn't leave her feeling any better. She'd give him a few days, allow him to start feeling stronger before she returned.

She and Tommy had grown closer over the past ten days. Now that he had regained his voice, he was full of questions and surprising insights.

When she wasn't spending time with Tommy, she focused on work, overseeing ops that were running smoothly, micromanaging everyone until Sal finally called her on it.

"What's going on, boss?"

She blew her bangs from her forehead. "What do you mean?"

"You look like you just had to drink a gallon of beet juice, you're on everyone's case and you're being a general pain in the rear."

"That bad, huh?"

"Worse. So give."

"Nothing important."

Sal eyed her shrewdly. "Would this 'nothing important' be a six-foot Delta who's been lying in a hospital bed for over a week and is probably crabby as all get-out?"

"It might be."

"Then go to him. Tell him how you feel."

Enough was enough. She'd put up with Sal's poking into her business, but he'd gone too far. "Are you forgetting who's the boss around here?"

"Don't play the boss card with me. You might be the boss, but you're still Jake's little sister, so it's my job to look out for you. Besides, you're my friend, and you're hurting."

With that, her temper deflated.

When she went to the hospital three days later, she was prepared to be patient with Caleb's moods. Of course he was anxious to get out of the hospital. She should have been more understanding. With that settled in her mind, she smiled. When she didn't find Caleb in his room, she didn't panic. He had probably been moved to a different room.

She found a nurse and asked what room Caleb had been transferred to.

The nurse looked surprised. "I'm sorry. Mr. Judd checked himself out."

"Did he leave a note...or anything?" Shelley worked to keep her voice neutral. There was nothing she could do about the churning in her gut.

"I'm sorry, ma'am," the young, fresh-faced nurse answered. "I don't know anymore."

"Did he talk with anyone? Say anything?"

"I'm sorry, ma'am," the nurse repeated, now looking a little harried. "I don't know anything about it. I was just assigned this floor today."

"Thank you."

Shelley turned, headed back down the hallway. She concentrated on putting one foot in front of the other. Maybe if she counted her steps, she wouldn't break down and bawl like a baby there in the middle of the hospital.

She took a step.

Another.

And another.

By the time she reached the bank of elevators, she had taken eighty-nine steps.

Well, what had she expected? The job was over. She'd learned from Caleb's cousin that Tommy was seeing a grief counselor a few times a week. Those responsible for his parents' deaths were in jail awaiting trial.

There was satisfaction in knowing that she would assist in putting the Kruises and Amachker and others behind bars for the rest of their lives. She was scheduled to give a deposition in another week.

The scandal of Alfred and Irene Kruise heading the largest crime organization on the East Coast had rocked Atlanta. Shelley figured she could dine out on sharing juicy tidbits for months to come if she were so inclined. She wasn't.

When working for the Metro PD, she'd seen her share of ugliness and corruption, but never had she witnessed anything like the operation the Kruises had run from their oh-so-genteel mansion.

The city was well rid of them.

In the meantime, she had plenty to keep her busy, including helping with the fund-raiser for Helping Hands. Shelley hadn't forgotten her promise to Pastor Monson. Like the pastor, she passionately believed in the work at the shelter.

The residents needed food, schooling and a host of other things, all of which cost money. With that reminder, she realized she was running late for a meeting with her sister-in-law at Belle Terre.

Jake and Dani had returned from a long honeymoon, and, judging by the glow in their eyes when they were together, were more in love than ever. A sharp pang of envy speared through Shelley before she braced herself against it. Dani and Jake deserved every bit of happiness they could find.

Three wives of Caleb's friends had started the ball rolling by spearheading a publicity campaign. With that and Dani's help, Shelley had high hopes that the event would be a success.

The drive to the antebellum mansion took Shelley out of the city and, at least for a while, out of her sullen thoughts. She found Dani in a huge room, probably a ballroom in a previous century, hanging pictures.

"Twenty-five hundred dollars?" Shelley asked in amazement, gazing at the watercolor hanging on a wall at the Barclay ancestral home. "For a child's drawing?"

A conspiratorial grin on her face, Dani Rabb nodded. "The more we charge, the more people will want to buy." Her voice was pure Southern, with little dips and pauses between each syllable. She could read from a phone book and mesmerize an audience with just the sound of her voice.

"It's a strange world you live in," Shelley said with bemused shake of her head. "A very strange world." Would anyone really pay over two thousand dollars for a drawing of sticklike trees and a ball of sun hanging over them?

"The important thing is that we make enough money to keep Helping Hands open. Besides, it's tax deductible."

"Amen," Pastor Monson said, joining them after he'd finished hanging another picture. "I just got a notice from the bank today, saying that we're three months behind in the mortgage. This benefit couldn't have come at a better time."

Shelley put aside her qualms and focused on helping Dani and the pastor hang the remainder of the children's art. "The senator has been great, agreeing to let us have the benefit at Belle Terre plus footing the bill for the catering."

Dani's face sobered. "It's been good for Daddy. And me."

Shelley nodded.

Dani didn't use her social connections for her own gain, but she had jumped at the chance to help raise money for Helping Hands. It had actually been her idea to frame the children's artwork and display it the night of the benefit, complete with discreet price tags. Now, if all went as planned, there should be money to spare to keep the shelter open.

By the end of the afternoon, all of the drawings were hung and priced. Shelley calculated that if even half of them sold, the shelter's books would be in the black for the next year, and that didn't even take into account what they hoped to raise at the benefit itself.

Unable to bear the uncertainty about Caleb a moment longer, she called his cousin. She and Shelley had grown closer over the past week as they conferred about the best way to help Tommy.

After a few pleasantries, Shelley asked about Caleb.

The other woman's surprise was evident in the long pause. "I thought… I assumed he'd told you," she said.

"Told me what?"

"Caleb returned to Afghanistan. He left two days ago."

Somehow Shelley managed to say goodbye. Her insides curled in on themselves, and she flattened her hand over her stomach, a futile attempt to smooth them out. Bands of steel seemed to crush her chest, constricting her lungs, and a deep rending shattered her heart. She forced out a breath even as the world seemed to buckle beneath her.

She had her answer as to why Caleb hadn't called: he'd never planned to.

EIGHTEEN

Shelley awoke with determined cheer.

The morning was the kind that made her think of a benediction from God: the sky a startling blue, the sun as shiny as a child's new toy and the humidity nearly bearable. The air wasn't crisp. Atlanta didn't do crisp, but it held the scent of the wild honeysuckle that grew in heady abandon this time of year.

She inhaled deeply and reminded herself that she had much to be grateful for. Just because Caleb hadn't called—and couldn't he have at least texted?—didn't mean that life wasn't good.

Mentally, she ticked off her blessings.

Jake looked happier than she'd seen him in years. Every day, she gave thanks for that. If not for Dani and the Lord, things could have turned out very differently.

She had gone an entire hour last night without thinking of Caleb every minute. Granted, thoughts of him had intruded every other minute, but it was progress all the same. Or so she told herself. Right now, she'd take what she could get.

The business was doing well, with clients lined up wanting to hire S&J Security Protection. The story of S&J's part in taking down Albert and Irene Kruise had upped the reputation of the business. Shelley had even been thinking of making Sal a partner and opening another office.

An unwelcome thought chased away her earlier optimism. Taryn Starks had called, wanting an interview regarding Shelley's part in toppling the Kruises' empire. When she had flatly refused, the reporter had switched directions. "What's this I hear about you organizing a benefit for a homeless shelter? I'd love to cover the affair, but I understand it's by invitation only." The hint hung heavy in the air.

"I'll see that you get one," Shelley promised reluctantly. Just because she didn't like the woman didn't mean that she could afford to turn away free publicity for Helping Hands.

"Thank you." Starks had all but purred the words. "I'll be there."

That had been two days ago. When Shelley told Dani, her sister-in-law had made a face. "I can't abide the woman any more than you can, but you're right. The publicity will be great."

Tonight was the big event, which promised to be wildly successful. Already donations were pouring in. Pastor Monson and his staff were ecstatic.

Shelley had a list of errands to run, courtesy of Dani. It turned out that Danielle Barclay Rabb was a tyrant when it came to a project she cared about. Dani had commandeered Jake and Shelley to check on the caterer.

"Lean on him if you have to and make sure he has the caviar I ordered," Dani had said, her honeyed tones at odds with the militant look in her eyes. "He had the nerve to try to convince me to accept imitation."

"Does that mean I get to break his arm?" Jake had asked, straight-faced.

"It means this is going to be a class act all the way and I'm not about to put up with an uppity caterer trying to pass off cheap stuff as the real thing."

"Your wife's scary," Shelley told Jake on the trip to the caterer's place of business.

"You're telling me. I asked if I could wear jeans and a T-shirt rather than a tux. She nearly took my head off." He shuddered in mock fear.

The happiness in his eyes, though, told a different story.

To her relief, he didn't ask about Caleb. The last thing she needed was for him to go all big brother on her.

The two of them completed their errands, and if her thoughts turned to a certain Delta soldier once or twice, she refused to admit it.

* * *

Caleb drew a long breath and considered what he'd done. Serving his country was the fabric of his being. Deciding to leave Delta was one of the most difficult decisions he had ever made, but he'd prayed for the Lord's guidance and knew it was right. For him. For Tommy. And maybe, just maybe, for Shelley, too.

The military had been his life for more than a decade. Fast-roping from helicopters. Tramping through crocodile-and-snake-infested waters. Running obstacle courses with an eighty-pound pack filled with extra ammo, flash bangs, slap charges and other assorted goodies strapped to his back. There'd been times when he'd thought he wouldn't make it.

Jumping from choppers into icy, filthy water where you didn't know what you'd encounter definitely separated the men from the boys.

Deltas were never content with good enough; their job was to succeed. Anything else was unacceptable.

Every step of the way, senior operatives graded you, busting your chops if you messed up even once. They never told you if you were passing or failing. They never even acknowledged you until and if you graduated.

There were plenty who didn't make it. There should be no shame in that, as the drop-out rate was astronomically high, but Caleb knew he would have beaten himself up over it every day for the rest of his life if he hadn't made the grade.

The work was excruciating, the pay miserable, the risks terrifying…and he wouldn't trade a minute of it for all the money on earth.

He hadn't been willing to leave it for Tricia and the glittery life she'd painted. At the time, he'd pictured himself doing the work he loved until age or injury made it impossible.

Being a Delta had fulfilled a deep-seated need in him to serve and protect, to fight for something bigger than himself. It had been the only place he'd ever really fit in. He would never regret those years, but it was time to move on.

He'd made a quick trip to Afghanistan. He owed it to his CO and to his buddies to tell them of his decision in person. Their disappointment was gratifying, but it didn't change his mind.

He'd served his country to the best of his ability; now it was time he was there for his family.

To his surprise, he didn't feel the wrenching loss he'd expected. Sure, he'd miss his buddies and the satisfaction of doing the job but his priorities had shifted. When he thought of Tommy waiting for him at their home, Caleb knew without a shadow of a doubt that he'd done the right thing. He'd enlisted because he wanted to make a difference. He could do that at home, in his own country. He didn't need to travel halfway around the world to make it a better place.

He was needed here. In Atlanta. He could serve wherever he was. He had some ideas on that, ones he wanted to run past Tommy. And Shelley.

Shelley.

His cousin had told him that Shelley had kept in touch with her about Tommy's progress. Did she wonder about Caleb, as well?

He hoped so.

Could he adjust to civilian life, trade storming an airplane after it had been taken by terrorists for playing football in the backyard on a Saturday afternoon? Which was what he'd just done with Tommy.

After they'd cleaned up, they sat at the kitchen table, him on the computer searching for a house and Tommy doing spelling words. He couldn't take his nephew back to the house where he'd seen his parents murdered.

Tommy tugged at Caleb's sleeve. "Uncle Caleb?"

Caleb looked up from his task. "Yeah, buddy?"

"I miss Shelley. I like her."

His nephew had good taste.

Caleb ruffled his hair. "I like her, too."

"Good."

Tommy was making progress in his therapy,

though there were bumps along the road. Tommy still woke several times a night with nightmares.

At the counselor's suggestion, Caleb attended some of the sessions as well, knowing that he had a part to play in the healing process. He also had his own healing to do. Part of that was forgiving himself.

He thought of Shelley, of his beautiful, vivacious bodyguard who'd touched a private place in his heart. Once she'd gotten over her fear of hurting him, Shelley had been good with Tommy. She'd rescued them both in so many ways.

She was quick-witted and optimistic, so full of vitality that she filled whatever space she happened to find herself in.

When he'd seen that she'd called, he'd wanted to return her call, but service was spotty at best where his unit was stationed. Besides, what he had to say needed to be said in person.

He thought of the valiant courage with which she approached life, the deep-seated faith that defined everything she did. He loved the way she laughed, how her smile lit her face from within and how she seemed to sense his every mood.

Caleb felt lighter, and, at the same time, more at peace than he had in years. Part of it was because Tommy was making progress, part because of Shelley.

Shelley.

Tough and feisty, compassionate and intelligent, she was everything he'd ever wanted in a woman. Her faith set her apart, giving her an air of quiet peace that somehow fit with the energy that was so much a part of her.

When Shelley had been missing, Caleb had been terrified he'd lost her forever. When he'd found her, he'd given thanks to the Lord, recognizing His hand in all that had happened. Cold fear had turned into something warm and solid.

That feeling had a name. Love.

He loved Shelley Rabb.

With her, he felt complete. She filled holes inside of him that he didn't even know were there.

Did she return his feelings? Sometimes he believed so, then he started to doubt himself. What if he were mistaken?

And, considering their time together had been spent trying to protect Tommy, not to mention searching for the truth about Michael and Grace's murders, maybe it was the intensity that he was picking up on rather than true, genuine emotion.

From the first, there had been an awareness between them. He'd done his best to ignore it, to focus on Tommy. The depth of his feelings for Shelley scared him nearly as much as had the idea that he might never see her again when Kruise and his men had held her.

He needed Shelley in every way. She had a way of soothing away the rough edges of a hard day and celebrating a good one. He considered the man he had been and who he was now…after Shelley. With her, he was more than he'd ever thought to be. She was his soul mate.

He wanted to share his life, himself, with her. And have her share her life, herself, with him. Would Shelley want to take on a man who came with so much baggage? He didn't know. The only thing he knew for sure was that he needed her as he'd never needed anyone else.

Love wasn't a fifty-fifty proposition. Michael had told him that. It's a 100 percent or nothing. Because you give everything and you get everything back.

He recalled how she'd looked the last time he'd seen her, so heartbreakingly beautiful that he'd ached with emotion. He'd wanted, *desperately*, to tell her of his feelings, but he hadn't been free then to tell her anything. Not until he'd settled his life.

Tonight was the benefit for Helping Hands. He planned on being there, where he would undertake the most important mission of his life: convincing Shelley that they belonged together.

When Shelley returned home after completing her errands, she had less than an hour to dress and make herself presentable. After showering, she slipped on the dress she'd bought for the benefit. Emerald green, it played up her eyes and complemented her hair. It draped softly over her hips to fall in gentle folds to her ankles. She studied her reflection in the mirror and decided she'd do.

Caleb's absence left a gaping hole in her heart, and she'd felt a part of her leave with him.

Before Caleb had left, Shelley had had a chance to watch him and Tommy together. Though man and boy were still wary of each other, the relationship seemed like it was on the right track.

It softened something of the sharp edges that could wrap around Caleb, the single-mindedness that could govern him at times. As for Tommy, he'd blossomed under the attention of his uncle. Shelley had no doubt that they would build something good of the seeds they'd planted.

She'd finally accepted that any relationship she and Caleb might have shared was over. Pain burned deep and hot in her veins. She told herself to get used to it, to go on without him. Examining what she felt for him was like probing a sore tooth.

It wasn't the first time someone she had loved had walked away from her. She'd survived her mother leaving her; she'd survive Caleb leaving, as well.

She'd kept busy, taking on more cases, working in her garden, preparing it for autumn. She sweated out her disappointment that came dangerously close to depression in the gym at the back of the house, but no matter how much she filled her days, she couldn't stop thinking of Caleb.

The days of shared effort aimed at a common goal, protecting Tommy, had brought them close in a way she'd never dreamed possible, but that was over. Had the feelings all been one-sided?

Caleb had a relationship to build with his nephew. That and Delta were his future. Shelley was but a very brief part of his past. After he'd settled Tommy, he'd returned to Delta. That was where his heart lay. Certainly not with her.

She tried to tell herself that she'd meet someone else. Even as the thought formed, she rejected it. The heart wants what the heart wants.

And hers wanted Caleb.

Even when he wasn't there to fill the space with his broad shoulders and strong, commanding presence, he managed to occupy her thoughts. Try as she would, she couldn't banish the pictures from her mind of her and Caleb growing old together, that ten, twenty years from now, she'd wake up in the middle of the night and he—her best friend, her husband—would be there, lying next to her, solid and warm and funny and kind.

A tiny sob hitched in her throat.

Pain and loss bruised her heart, but she refused to give in to them. Despite the heartache, she felt stronger, more able to deal with the past.

She would always regret what had happened with Jeffrey, but she was learning to accept that it hadn't been her fault. Would she have become as strong and accepting of the past if Caleb had not come into her life?

She didn't think so. She had a life, a good one. Work she loved, a brother and his new wife, both of whom she adored, and the faith that had always sustained her.

In the meantime, she had a job to do tonight. Dani had asked her to be there to help schmooze, as her friend put it.

"I'm no good at that stuff," Shelley had protested.

"And you think I am? You need to be there," Dani insisted. "I'm liable to get on my soapbox and tell everyone to pony up." She rolled her eyes. "Think how that would go over."

Shelley had agreed, which was how she found herself in a dress that cost the equivalent of a month's mortgage. She'd rationalized the splurge by reminding herself that it was for a good cause. Besides, she needed the boost to her ego.

Tentatively, she touched her hair, unaccustomed to the slicked-back style that left her face unframed. She'd deepened her eye shadow and had dabbed peach lip gloss over her mouth. She felt like a little girl playing dress-up in her mother's clothes and makeup.

Though Jake and Dani had offered her a ride,

she preferred to drive herself. After she did her share of schmoozing, she planned on making an early escape. Once again, she thought of Caleb. Disappointment wallowed in her stomach. She'd hoped they'd be attending tonight's festivities together.

Get over it. It wasn't meant to be.

The smile she'd plastered on her lips felt as phony as the rest of her, but she kept it in place and walked into the Belle Terre mansion with her head held high. The event's venue was one of the few stately homes in Atlanta to have remained in the same family since before the War Between the States. An invitation to Belle Terre was more sought after than one to the governor's mansion.

That alone was enough to attract the wealthy and influential. She prayed those same people could be persuaded to part with some of their money to support Helping Hands.

She stood poised at the entrance of the marble-floored ballroom.

The massive room dripped with crystal, the guests with jewels. The scent of expensive perfume wafted through the air, making her wish for the clean, fresh smell of a Georgia morning. The artificially cooled air had nothing on the chill in her heart as she recalled Caleb's promise that he'd be there.

Shelley sucked in a breath. *You can do this.*

Jake, with Dani at his side, gave a wide grin

when he caught sight of her. "Looking good, little sis." He wrapped an arm around her and hugged her, lifting her off her feet.

"You clean up pretty good yourself." She turned to Dani and kissed her cheek. "You look great. Marriage agrees with you"

Her sister-in-law was stunning in an ice-blue gown, but it was the pure happiness in her eyes that made her radiant.

At the obvious love that passed between her brother and his bride, Shelley once again pushed aside an unwelcome spurt of envy. Unbidden, memories of Caleb found their way into her mind.

She chided herself for her wayward feelings. This evening was to raise money for Helping Hands, not to wallow in might-have-beens.

"I'm the happiest woman on the face of the earth." Dani smiled brilliantly and tucked her arm inside that of her husband.

Shelley made the introductions as Pastor Monson joined the threesome.

"We can't thank you and your father enough for making this possible," he said to Dani.

Dani shook her head. "It was all Daddy's doing. When he heard where the money was going, he couldn't do enough. It's been tough, what with learning about my mother and all." Her voice turned husky, and she cleared her throat. Sadness moved in and out of her eyes, quick as a wink. "He needed a project he could sink his teeth into."

Shelley watched as Jake drew Dani closer, a strong, comforting arm around her shoulders.

In protecting Dani from a stalker, Jake had uncovered the truth about Dani's mother's disappearance. Learning what had happened to her mother hadn't been easy, but Dani had taken the news with the kind of grace and strength Shelley had come to expect of her. There was no doubt in her mind that her brother had chosen a winner.

"Dani's father is a stand-up guy," Jake said. "He's already making plans to make this a yearly event in honor of his late wife."

"I know my mother would have been proud," Dani said in a steadier voice.

There was a moment of silence before she added, "She always had a soft spot for those in need."

"Making this a yearly event is the best news I could hear," the pastor said.

Jake turned toward Shelley. "Can I have a dance with my favorite sister?"

She smiled, but something in his eyes alerted her that this wasn't a simple request for a dance. "Of course."

Jake led her to the dance floor. "What's going on with you and Caleb?" There was no beating about the bush for her brother.

She turned up the wattage on her smile and prayed it passed Jake's scrutiny. "What do you mean?"

"I mean, *what's going on between you and Caleb?*"

Shelley recognized his big-brother act and knew she had to come clean. "Nothing. Absolutely nothing." She tried for a light tone but failed miserably, and she knew her smile was more bittersweet than happy.

"I'll strangle him," Jake growled.

"You'll do no such thing. Caleb was a client. That's all."

"You never could lie to me," he chastised gently.

He was right. She was a terrible liar. Always had been. She wanted to weep in his arms but stiffened her backbone and reminded herself that she was a grown woman, not Jake's helpless little sister.

"Are you okay?" he asked in such a tender voice that she nearly cried.

"No. But I'll figure out how to be." She summoned a smile. "Tonight's not about me. And you've got a bride who's waiting for you."

A smile slid over Jake's face. "That I do. We'll talk later," he promised.

Not if she could help it.

It was then that Shelley noticed Taryn Starks chatting up a society maven. The reporter's black dress and matching evening jacket did nothing to flatter her sallow complexion, Shelley mused, and then chided herself for the catty thought. Starks carried a large bag, at odds with the tiny evening purses most of the women favored. Probably held a laptop or tablet.

Jake returned her to where the pastor and Dani waited. His bride hooked an arm through Shelley's. "Can I borrow your sister? I need her help." As they wove through the crowd, Dani said, "You look fantastic."

"So do you."

Dani preened a bit, while her lips curved in a wry smile. "Now that we've agreed that we both look fabulous, let's get to work."

When Dani said work, she meant it. She began by introducing Shelley to the mayor and his wife.

"You've done yourself proud," the lady, who wore a diamond choker that probably cost more than Shelley's first car, said. "It's a lovely affair. And you can be sure that the mayor and I will be adding our support to the cause."

"Thank you for your generosity," Shelley murmured.

By the time she'd gone through five more meet-and-greets, she felt she had the patter down. After an hour of making nice to the city fathers and other dignitaries, she gave Dani a pleading look and made her escape.

With a sigh of relief on her lips, Shelley slipped

off to an alcove, where she could view the party but enjoy a brief respite at the same time. She looked at the ridiculous high-heeled shoes she'd probably never wear again, and leaned against the wall. She took a deep breath and released it, savoring the relative quiet after the noise of the ballroom. Despite the heartache that thoughts of Caleb brought, she knew a quiet satisfaction of having contributed to a good cause.

She let her gaze take in the scene and thought this must have been how it was nearly two hundred years ago, elegantly dressed men and women dancing in the opulent ballroom. Out of the corner of her eye, she saw Taryn Starks move to the buffet tables.

Shelley walked back into the ballroom, Something about the reporter's actions caught Shelley's attention. She shifted to get a better look at the woman and saw her stoop behind one of the tables. A few seconds later, she stood, then moved to a second table, and repeated the process.

What was going on?

Shelley moved closer. "Leaving so early?" she asked.

"I've got a deadline," Starks said. Perspiration sheened her forehead. Her tongue darted out and rimmed her upper lip.

That plus the telltale tightening at Starks's eyes and the corners of her mouth alerted Shelley that the woman wasn't telling the truth.

"I've got to go. You have no right to hold me."

Tiny red lines showed in her eyes. Anger? Shelley wondered. Or fear…?

"And here you were so anxious to come tonight, even calling me up and angling for an invitation." Shelley kept her voice calm. If what she suspected were true, everyone in the ballroom was in danger.

Shelley clamped her hand over the other woman's wrist, forcing her hand open and caught her breath at what Starks held in her hand. A detonator. Fury burned through her, but she couldn't act on it. Not as long as Starks had the detonator.

Starks pushed Shelley backward and wrenched her arm free, but not before Shelley grabbed the detonator.

Dani joined them at that moment. "Shelley, what's going on?"

Before Shelley could warn her sister-in-law to stay back, Starks yanked Dani to her. From the pocket of her evening jacket, she pulled out a small but deadly-looking knife.

Both Shelley and Jake had taught Dani some rudimentary moves in self-defense, but she was no match for a woman with a knife.

"Stay back," Starks warned. "Give me the detonator or I'll slit her throat."

"Don't do it, Shelley," Dani cried. "You can't give it to her. She'll kill us all."

NINETEEN

Caleb spotted Shelley and Dani at the far side of the ballroom. It looked as if Shelley was arguing with another woman. The reporter, the one Shelley didn't like.

When Starks grabbed Dani, Caleb sprinted to the scene, making sure he stayed out of Starks's field of vision. By now, he understood that this wasn't some simple disagreement, but that Dani was in real peril. He understood Shelley well enough to know that she'd rather it be her who was in danger.

"Nobody's been hurt," Shelley said. "You can still walk out of here." A professional to the core, she didn't react by so much as a blink when she saw him moving quietly into position behind the reporter.

"You don't get it, do you?" Starks screamed. "I'm as good as dead now. Kruise doesn't tolerate screw-ups."

Caleb swallowed the sharp hiss of breath that

threatened to escape. It made a horrible kind of sense. Kruise had bragged that he had reporters in his pocket as well as law enforcement officials.

Out of his peripheral vision, Caleb saw Jake flank the woman's other side. A hand signal was all it took to communicate between the two warriors. Caleb gave an infinitesimal nod to Shelley.

"Just don't hurt her," Shelley pleaded with Starks, a ploy he recognized to distract the reporter. "She's done nothing to you. I'll give you the detonator." She made as though to do just that when Caleb and Jake made their move.

Jake pulled Dani out of Starks's grasp while Caleb wrestled the knife from her. With surprising strength, she put up a good fight, clawing at his face until he pinned her arms behind her back. Caleb handed the knife to Shelley.

"She brought along some party favors," Shelley said. "I think we'll find it's plastic explosive or something similar."

"Any idea where?" he asked quietly.

"Check under the tables," she said and hitched her chin at the food-laden tables, before turning her attention to the group of curious guests who had gathered around the scene.

"Take care of her," Caleb said with a nod in Jake's direction.

"With pleasure." Jake took charge of Starks while Caleb went to scope out what the reporter had placed beneath the tables. After spotting two compact bombs, he returned and gave the reporter a dark look. "You're done. Just like your boss."

Starks had quit struggling, but her eyes hardened with defiance as she directed her glare at Caleb and Shelley. "You think you've won. Kruise can get to you and your family anytime, anywhere.

"He has people up and down the Eastern Seaboard. You may have won the battle, but you won't win the war. Mark my words."

"If you know what's good for you, you'll turn state's evidence and testify against him," Dani, ever the deputy DA, said.

A gleam appeared in Starks's eyes. "You'll cut me a deal?"

Dani was saved from answering when her father threaded his way through the growing crowd. "I've called the police," he said and then looked at Starks in contempt. "I've always thought you were sleazy, but I never knew just how corrupt you actually were."

Two policemen showed up and hauled the woman away.

"It's over now," Caleb said.

"Is it?" Shelley asked, worrying her bottom lip. "You heard what she said."

"We'll deal with whatever happens. Together."

He'd never meant anything more. He and Shelley belonged together.

The ballroom was cleared, and bomb disposal units arrived. Shrill screams and cries had punctuated the night as the guests became aware that they'd narrowly escaped an explosion.

Though the benefit had ended early, Shelley knew that the guests, once the initial panic was over, were thrilled at being present at such an event and would be more generous than ever with their donations to Helping Hands. In that sense, the evening was a total success.

What about for her? Caleb had arrived just in time, but all that meant was that he'd fulfilled his promise.

She and Caleb, along with Jake, Dani and Dani's father, had been asked to remain outside while police searched the house for further bombs.

There, in the gardens flanking the mansion, with the scent of late summer roses heavy in the air, Shelley looked her fill at Caleb. Resplendent in a dark tuxedo that perfectly fit his powerful, rangy build, he stood there, more heartstoppingly handsome than ever. She ached with wanting.

He looked as though he had stepped outside a fairy tale storybook, his potent masculinity scattering her thoughts. She wanted to lift a hand to cup his stubbled cheek but resisted the temptation. Her senses were off-kilter and couldn't be trusted.

He'd lost weight in the past few weeks, the angles of his face more prominent, the bones sharply defined. Her heart panged. She stared up at him, her muscles tensing in painful anticipation. She wasn't prepared for the onslaught of emotions that poured through her.

It held her in its grip for a beat in time. Yet another beat passed before she could pry her tongue loose from the roof of her mouth. She could feel the tension skimming around the edges of her system.

At the same moment, the world seemed to shift as memories cut through her mind: Caleb's lips upon hers as he kissed her oh-so-gently; Caleb wrapping a bandage around her ankle; Caleb fighting alongside her.

"Starks was right," Shelley said thickly. "Kruise has a long reach."

"I told you that we'd deal with it. Together."

Maybe she'd just wanted to hear him say it again, but the words settled around her heart with quiet warmth.

"I didn't expect to see you." With adrenaline still thrumming through her, her voice was scarcely more than a whiff of breath.

The words trembled between them, turning the air husky with all she wanted to say and didn't, all he could have said and hadn't.

He stepped closer and reached out to touch the sensitive skin at her temple. "I told you I'd be here." A whisper of a smile brushed his lips.

His words threw her off balance, and Shelley worked to regain her focus. She closed her eyes in memory of his touch.

"Didn't you think I'd make good on my promise?"

"It wasn't that. I only meant I figured you'd be busy with Tommy." She knew that the healing process wouldn't be accomplished overnight and that Tommy would probably need long-term counseling.

"Tommy is doing great. He has a way to go, but he's...we're...getting there." A line dug between his brows. "It's been rough. I won't deny it. But we'll make it." Caleb paused, his gaze searching hers. "I'm adopting him."

"I'm glad." Shelley winced at the banal reply. Such a life-changing event for both boy and man deserved more.

For the life of her, though, she couldn't think of anything else to say. She felt as tongue-tied as a young girl at her first school dance and just as awkward.

"Shelley." There was a world of intimacy in the single word. He brushed his fingers along her jawbone, then beneath her chin to lift it. His face was but scant inches from her own, and her senses leaped at his nearness.

The warmth of his hand, the breadth of his shoulders, the husky caress of his voice—all were achingly familiar and infinitely dear.

She wanted to put distance between them but was powerless to move. He smelled of soap and lime, the combination a pleasant contrast to the overly perfumed air. It was all she could do not to press her face against his neck and inhale deeply.

"I've missed you." Love, sweet and tender, wrapped its way around her at the warmth in his eyes.

But though his words moved her, she couldn't forget that she hadn't heard from him in over a month. She thought about denying her feelings, then accepted that she'd never been any good at playing games, even if she'd wanted to. Which she didn't.

She needed to think clearly, to process the gamut of emotions roiling through her, and she couldn't do that when he gazed at her with such undisguised affection. "Missed me so much that you didn't have a minute to call, tell me how you were?" Her voice snipped, sharp as the shears she'd used to prune back her roses, and she winced.

"I've missed you, too," she added more softly.

"I'm sorry I didn't call."

"Why didn't you?" The snip was back.

"I made a quick trip to Afghanistan, then I was busy dealing with Tommy, helping him adjust to a new place." He took a breath, as though readying himself for a hard truth. "But that's not the real reason."

She wondered if she wanted to ask the question and decided she had to know. "What is it?"

"I've been doing some heavy-duty thinking. About what I want from life. For myself. For Tommy." He paused. "I've left Delta."

Whatever she'd expected, it wasn't that. "Delta's your life."

"Not anymore. I've put in nine years. I don't regret a minute of it. But it's time I started focusing on family. I want a home, not just a home base."

"That's great," she said and meant it.

"There's something else."

"What?" Her voice was a scratchy whisper.

"I should say there's *someone* else." The vulnerability in his eyes caused her heart to twist. "You."

"Me?" Her voice had morphed to a squeak.

"You. I want you to be part of my life." He swallowed hard. "You and Tommy are the first thing I think of when I wake up and the last thing I think of before I go to bed."

"Tommy and me? Together?"

His nod was emphatic. "Together. That's what I want for us. To be together."

"Like a family?"

"Just like a family."

She got that feeling in her chest, the one that told her everything was all right, the one that was happiness.

He took her hand, linked her fingers with his own. "I need a helpmate to start my new life. I want to work with the Wounded Warrior Project. There're so many returning soldiers who need help."

"Like Jake," she said softly.

He nodded. "Like Jake. And all the other men and women who came home broken, if not in body, then in spirit."

Cartwheels of joy tumbled in her heart. At the same time, her heart seemed to be beating in her throat. How was that possible? She wanted to fill the silence but wasn't certain she could speak. It felt as though all the oxygen had been sucked from the room. She paused a moment to take it all in. "You want me to join you?"

"I know you won't give up your business. I wouldn't want you to. But in your spare time, maybe you could work with me."

"There's nothing I'd like better."

"I love you," he said, the simplicity of the words not detracting a whit from their meaning.

She held the declaration to her heart, feeling the love and devotion in the three words. He folded her into his arms. There, nestled against his chest, she heard the beating of his heart, felt his breath in her hair. She longed to stay right where she was. She breathed in the scent of him, taking comfort in the familiarity of it.

Dozens of feelings poured through her.

Fear that she'd never see him again.

And love. There was no point in denying it. She loved Caleb Judd. With that, her breathing turned raspy.

"Oh, Caleb..."

"Shh. Just let me hold you," he murmured against her hair.

She'd have been happy to let him hold her forever. He bent his head to brush his lips over hers. The world melted away. All that mattered was the touch of Caleb's mouth to hers.

The sweet, tender embrace seemed to go on forever.

When he finally lifted his head, his warm gaze never leaving hers, a rush of feeling poured through her. And she knew she had been waiting all her life for this moment, this man.

Caleb took her hands. "We each have plenty of bad stuff behind us, and we can't help that some of it's still sticking to us, but it's helped make us who we are. And, for that, I'm grateful. Grateful that whatever happened brought you and me together."

He was looking at her the way she'd always dreamed he would. With everything he was feeling and nothing held back. With unmistakable love. The forever-and-ever kind. The kind that would see them through both good times and bad.

Caleb dropped to one knee. "Shelley Rabb, will you marry me?" He slipped a hand into his pocket and pulled out a small square box. He opened it, revealing a simple band with a gleaming diamond. "Be my wife. My helpmate. You are everything to me. You make me happier than I have a right to expect."

Her heart in her throat, Shelley managed to get out a single word. "Yes."

He slipped the ring on her fourth finger, stood, and suddenly her feet were off the ground as he swept her into his arms. Her head felt light, her heart full. All of her senses came alive as he slanted his lips over hers.

"I think I knew from the start you were the only woman for me, but I couldn't let myself feel what I wanted to. Tommy had to come first." He tipped her chin up until their gazes met. "You are everything I ever wanted. Loyal. Strong. Intelligent. And so beautiful you take my breath away."

"Don't forget nearly perfect." Her grin acknowledged her own imperfections.

He leaned down, once more settling his lips over hers. Gently. So very gently. Softly. So very softly. All of her doubts scattered at the press of his lips to hers in a kiss so tender that it made her throat ache and her toes curl.

"You take my breath away," he said. "You

always have. Even when I was crazy with worry, I knew that you were important in a way no other woman has been or will ever be. I didn't want to admit it. It wasn't supposed to happen like that, but it was there staring me in the face the whole time."

"It was the same for me," she confessed. "Almost from the first."

"You are my heart."

She went still. "And you are mine." She set the tears free.

He thumbed away the glistening drops that trailed down her cheeks. "Thank you."

"For what?"

"For helping me find myself."

"You were never lost." She skimmed her knuckles over his cheek. "I love you, Caleb Judd." She took his hand, placed it over her heart. "I will love you forever."

"And ever."

* * * * *

Dear Reader,

I hope you enjoyed Shelley and Caleb's story. As with so many of us, the course of love did not run smoothly for them. And perhaps that is the lesson. Love isn't supposed to be a smooth path. It is bumpy and messy and full of detours and, in Shelley and Caleb's case, dangerous twists. But all those things combined to bring them together in the end.

My own "love path" has not always run smoothly. My real-life hero and husband of forty-two years and I love each other dearly. We have survived teenagers, unemployment, illness and, did I say teenagers? Sometimes, in frustration, we lash out at each other. And then we remember the vows we made, the covenants with each other and the Lord. When we invite Him into our lives, we rediscover our love and our commitment to each other and to Him.

I hope your love path includes the Lord.

Always,
Jane M. Choate

LARGER-PRINT BOOKS!

GET 2 FREE LARGER-PRINT NOVELS PLUS 2 FREE MYSTERY GIFTS

Love Inspired®

Larger-print novels are now available...

LILP15

REQUEST YOUR FREE BOOKS!
2 FREE WHOLESOME ROMANCE NOVELS
IN LARGER PRINT
PLUS 2
FREE
MYSTERY GIFTS

HEARTWARMING™

Wholesome, tender romances

YES! Please send me 2 FREE Harlequin® Heartwarming Larger-Print novels and my 2 FREE mystery gifts (gifts worth about $10). After receiving them, if I don't wish to receive any more books, I can return the shipping statement marked "cancel." If I don't cancel, I will receive 4 brand-new larger-print novels every month and be billed just $5.24 per book in the U.S. or $5.99 per book in Canada. That's a savings of at least 19% off the cover price. It's quite a bargain! Shipping and handling is just 50¢ per book in the U.S. and 75¢ per book in Canada.* I understand that accepting the 2 free books and gifts places me under no obligation to buy anything. I can always return a shipment and cancel at any time. Even if I never buy another book, the two free books and gifts are mine to keep forever.

161/361 IDN GHX2

Name	(PLEASE PRINT)	
Address		Apt. #
City	State/Prov.	Zip/Postal Code

Signature (if under 18, a parent or guardian must sign)

Mail to the **Reader Service:**
IN U.S.A.: P.O. Box 1867, Buffalo, NY 14240-1867
IN CANADA: P.O. Box 609, Fort Erie, Ontario L2A 5X3

* Terms and prices subject to change without notice. Prices do not include applicable taxes. Sales tax applicable in N.Y. Canadian residents will be charged applicable taxes. Offer not valid in Quebec. This offer is limited to one order per household. Not valid for current subscribers to Harlequin Heartwarming larger-print books. All orders subject to credit approval. Credit or debit balances in a customer's account(s) may be offset by any other outstanding balance owed by or to the customer. Please allow 4 to 6 weeks for delivery. Offer available while quantities last.

Your Privacy—The Reader Service is committed to protecting your privacy. Our Privacy Policy is available online at www.ReaderService.com or upon request from the Reader Service.

We make a portion of our mailing list available to reputable third parties that offer products we believe may interest you. If you prefer that we not exchange your name with third parties, or if you wish to clarify or modify your communication preferences, please visit us at www.ReaderService.com/consumerschoice or write to us at Reader Service Preference Service, P.O. Box 9062, Buffalo, NY 14240-9062. Include your complete name and address.

HWI5

YES! Please send me **The Montana Mavericks Collection** in Larger Print. This collection begins with 3 FREE books and 2 FREE gifts (gifts valued at approx. $20.00 retail) in the first shipment, along with the other first 4 books from the collection! If I do not cancel, I will receive 8 monthly shipments until I have the entire 51-book Montana Mavericks collection. I will receive 2 or 3 FREE books in each shipment and I will pay just $4.99 US/ $5.89 CDN for each of the other four books in each shipment, plus $2.99 for shipping and handling per shipment.*If I decide to keep the entire collection, I'll have paid for only 32 books, because 19 books are FREE! I understand that accepting the 3 free books and gifts places me under no obligation to buy anything. I can always return a shipment and cancel at any time. My free books and gifts are mine to keep no matter what I decide.

263 HCN 2404   463 HCN 2404

Name	(PLEASE PRINT)	
Address		Apt. #
City	State/Prov.	Zip/Postal Code

Signature (if under 18, a parent or guardian must sign)

Mail to the **Reader Service:**
IN U.S.A.: P.O. Box 1867, Buffalo, NY 14240-1867
IN CANADA: P.O. Box 609, Fort Erie, Ontario L2A 5X3

* Terms and prices subject to change without notice. Prices do not include applicable taxes. Sales tax applicable in N.Y. Canadian residents will be charged applicable taxes. This offer is limited to one order per household. All orders subject to approval. Credit or debit balances in a customer's account(s) may be offset by any other outstanding balance owed by or to the customer. Please allow 4 to 6 weeks for delivery. Offer available while quantities last. Offer not available to Quebec residents.

MMLPBPA15

READERSERVICE.COM

Manage your account online!

- Review your order history
- Manage your payments
- Update your address

We've designed the
Reader Service website
just for you.

Enjoy all the features!

- Discover new series available to you, and read excerpts from any series.
- Respond to mailings and special monthly offers.
- Connect with favorite authors at the blog.
- Browse the Bonus Bucks catalog and online-only exculsives.
- Share your feedback.

Visit us at:
ReaderService.com